DONUTHEAD

OTHER DELL YEARLING BOOKS YOU WILL ENJOY

HOW TO EAT FRIED WORMS, *Thomas Rockwell*

VARJAK PAW, *SF Said*

THE PHANTOM TOLLBOOTH, *Norton Juster*

WITH LOVE FROM SPAIN, MELANIE MARTIN, *Carol Weston*

PURE DEAD BRILLIANT, *Debi Gliori*

THE LEGACY OF GLORIA RUSSELL, *Sheri Gilbert*

LIZARD MUSIC, *D. Manus Pinkwater*

BELLE PRATER'S BOY, *Ruth White*

TROUT AND ME, *Susan Shreve*

HOW TíA LOLA CAME TO ~~VISIT~~ STAY, *Julia Alvarez*

DELL YEARLING BOOKS are designed especially to entertain and enlighten young people. Patricia Reilly Giff, consultant to this series, received her bachelor's degree from Marymount College and a master's degree in history from St. John's University. She holds a Professional Diploma in Reading and a Doctorate of Humane Letters from Hofstra University. She was a teacher and reading consultant for many years, and is the author of numerous books for young readers.

DONUTHEAD

Sue Stauffacher

A Dell Yearling Book

Published by
Dell Yearling
an imprint of
Random House Children's Books
a division of Random House, Inc.
New York

Visit us on the Web! www.randomhouse.com/kids

Educators and librarians, for a variety of teaching tools, visit us at
www.randomhouse.com/teachers

ISBN: 0-440-41934-4

Reprinted by arrangement with Alfred A. Knopf Books for Young Readers

Printed in the United States of America

June 2005

10 9 8 7 6 5 4 3 2

OPM

This book is dedicated with love to my sons, Max and Walter Gilles, who have taught me that the most important thing is to be kind.

The test of our progress is not whether we add more to the abundance of those who have much; it is whether we provide enough for those who have too little.

—Franklin Delano Roosevelt

DONUTHEAD

CHAPTER ONE

Just the Facts

My name, if you must know, is Franklin Delano Donuthead.

Try saying *that* in a room full of fifth graders if you think names will never hurt you.

The Donuthead part comes from way back, from my great-great-great-great-grandfather who came to the United States during the famous turnip famine. Of course he didn't speak a lick of English. His Russian name was something like Donotscked. Somehow, when he came out of the ferry office at Ellis Island with a piece of paper in his hand, he was a Donuthead.

So, basically, I come from a long line of suffering Russian Donutheads.

All the suffering could have been avoided if it weren't for Washington Irving, this very famous writer who recorded the events of his life in his journal. One day, he wrote about these little balls of sweetened dough he liked fried up in hog fat. He called them dough nuts. Because, you see, the very first dough-nuts were shaped like lumpy brown walnuts.

If only he'd stuck with the name the Dutch people gave them. They were the ones who created them, anyway. They called them olykoeks. If he had called them olykoeks, my life would have been very different, I assure you.

Then again, with my luck, I would have been named Franklin Delano Olykoekhead.

My mother is a major major fan of our thirty-second president. She likes to listen to the radio addresses that Franklin Delano Roosevelt gave when he came into office during the Great Depression. Believe it or not, she listens to them in her van during her workday. She has them all on tape.

"If FDR could rise above a life-threatening illness to become president of the United States, then you should be able to rise above the curse of a name like Donuthead to at least play third base for the New York Yankees," my mother says.

I think this is very unfair. Your mother gives you a name when you're all red and screaming and you have a pounding headache. You're not really in a position to question the "future" situation.

Now that I am eleven, I have pretty much accepted my life. I'm a Russian Donuthead who's named after a great handicapped president.

In some twisted way, this all makes sense. Because, you see, I too am handicapped. Yes, one side of my body is shorter than the other. My mother says this is my imagination, but I am here to tell you that a tape measure does not lie.

"Maybe you're just growing from side to side," she says. "One side first and then the other."

While this may be possible, I think it's highly unlikely. I have found no evidence to support this theory. Currently, there is an eight-tenths-of-an-inch difference between my left arm and my right arm, and a four-tenths-of-an-inch difference between my left leg and my right leg. Just yesterday, when I measured my legs after school, I found my toe creeping closer to the five. I am preparing myself mentally to have legs that look like they belong on two different bodies. Both my left arm and my left leg are longer. At this rate, I'm going to have to go to one of those special stores to be fitted for my Sunday suits. Soon, I'll be buying shoes with one high heel.

All my mother cares about is how this will affect my ability to play third base for the New York Yankees. I keep telling her that with my athletic ability, I'd be lucky if they hired me to chalk out the field. I think it's so pathetic how parents are always trying to transfer their dreams onto their kids.

So far, I've just focused on staying alive. If I didn't know there was an astonishingly high probability that I would live through each day—given my age, general health, and relatively high standard of living—I would not get out of bed in the morning.

I avoid motor vehicles whenever possible. According to the National Safety Department, this is by far the most likely way to die as a kid. I also avoid all bodies of water (drowning's number two), and anything that would cause a death-inducing accident (number three). This could be, oh, say, being hit in the temple by a hard grounder down the third base line. In addition, I never play with matches or firearms; never climb trees, ladders, or fences; change the smoke detector batteries every three months; do not drink liquids that are stored under the sink or put any plastic bags over my head.

Gloria Nelots, the chief statistician for the National Safety Department in Washington, has already offered me a job when I graduate from college—if I should live that long. She and I talk at least once a week.

• • •

Me: Good morning, Gloria.

Gloria: What is it now, Franklin?

Me: My school is planning a field trip to a working farm.

Gloria: And . . .

Me: I was just wondering . . . what is the likelihood of me being crushed by a moving tractor?

Gloria: Remote.

Me: Trapped in a hay silo and suffocated by grain?

Gloria: They don't make percentages that small.

Me: Can mad cow disease be transmitted by saliva? I mean, if a cow licks me, and . . .

Gloria: Franklin, you would have to eat it, and since you never touch red meat . . .

Me: Gloria, I think you should know our school bus does not have seat belts.

Gloria: I'll get someone on it right away, Franklin.

Me: It's Bus Number 987 in the Pelican View School District. In addition, I think the rear tires are overinflated, causing premature baldness. I was just wondering, Gloria . . .

Gloria: You won't get a note from me, Franklin, if that's what you're angling for. I think it's perfectly safe for you to go to the farm.

Me: Well, obviously, I'm concerned for the safety of all the students, not just myself. Recently, I noticed that several children have been coming to school with their shoes untied. These are young children, Gloria . . .

Gloria: Franklin?

Me: Yes?

Gloria: Do you ever think about girls?

Me: Girls, Gloria?

Gloria: I think it would be better for your health if you thought about girls rather than disasters. Stress plays a major role in the leading causes of death in this nation.

Well, let me tell you, I didn't have anything to say to that. I just had to hang up right then. After all, Gloria is a girl. How could I tell her that girls filled me with so much stress they ought to come with warning labels?

Girls I do not understand. Girls cannot be quantified in any way. The laws of mathematics, physics, and chemistry do not apply to anything wearing a barrette or a gold bracelet. Unless, of course, it's not real gold. Then you may witness a green ring on the skin resulting from the interaction between base metals and the acids in both perspiration and the atmosphere.

The only thing that frightens me more than girls is the Pelican View Basketball Team. We don't have the full complement of sports teams like you get in middle school. Just a basketball team and a baseball team.

Anybody who wants to can be on the team. You can have the mental fitness of a pretzel, and the grace of a station wagon on black ice, and Coach Jablonski still has to take you on the team. In winter, I was being terrorized by the basketball team. Come spring, it would be the baseball team. For some reason, all the boys who like to pound on sensitive, asymmetrical guys like me are also attracted to Pelican View sports teams.

There's one other factor in my safety profile that I should mention. I am fatherless. My mother is husbandless. This is both devastating and out of my control. I have mentioned to my mother that coming from a single-parent home puts me at a disproportionately high risk for all sorts of life-threatening behaviors, like alcohol and drug abuse, depression and anger management issues, and being abducted by kidnappers on the rare evening she has to work late.

When I ask her what she intends to do about this, my mother gets rather testy. "Franklin, you gave a medical questionnaire to the last guy. Remember? At the door?"

The medical questionnaire was for the mechanic she met on the Internet. I thought it necessary to take a few extra precautions. Normally, a brief interview is sufficient.

"I cannot understand why you object to learning about a person's overall state of health," I said.

We were having dinner together and it was my turn to be chef. I'd chosen a dish composed mostly of dark orange and green vegetables for their antioxidant properties. Though I'd made it myself, my mother was dissecting her serving as if it were a frog she'd found flattened at the side of the road.

"When the Lepners bought their dog," I continued calmly, "they had a licensed veterinarian check his eyes, his legs, even his hips. The way I see it, a father is an investment. You don't want to put all your energy into getting one and then have him keel over from a heart attack two years down the line."

My mother flipped over a slice of sweet potato and inspected the underside. "For your information, *I'm* not looking for a father. And I'd rather leave some things to chance, to . . . I don't know . . . the great unknowable."

She skewered her sweet potato and popped it into her

mouth, grimacing. "And the Lepners' dog got run over by the recycling truck, in case you've forgotten!"

Unfortunately, this was true, and it did not strengthen my argument. The Lepners lived next door to us. Bernie Lepner was my full-time neighbor and my sometimes I-have-to-play-with-you-because-my-mother-says-so friend. Which meant I had to go to the funeral. Which was held at a pet cemetery. Needless to say, I bathed in a hydrogen peroxide solution when I got home.

"I think we should give the health inspector another chance," I said, trying to steer the conversation back to the subject of suitable fathers.

My mother got up from the table and began energetically scraping her casserole into the garbage. "He had blue lips. I wasn't attracted," she said.

"Is that all you can object to? You're a girl, for heaven's sake! You should know we can change that."

"Look, Franklin, when you're ready to date, you can choose girls however you want. You might buy them wrapped in plastic from Toys "R" Us for all I know. I'm just looking for someone who likes the same things I do, someone who might find you . . . interesting."

She opened the fridge, pulled out a container of yogurt and an apple, and sat back down with me. I tried hard not to let this injure my culinary pride.

"And yes, I want someone I'm attracted to." There was a long silence while she sawed her apple into slices and spooned yogurt over them.

"Do you think my real father has children by now?" I asked.

"Now don't go calling him your *real* father, Franklin. He didn't want to be a father. He was a sperm donor."

"But he might be a father now!"

"And the Lepners' dog might be alive with a litter of puppies."

"Baron was a male."

"You know what I mean."

Unfortunately, I did know what she meant. My mother meant that some questions have no answers. Of course I had a father. Everyone does. But I also didn't have a father. Because the man whose genes were coursing around inside me had never met my mother and he'd certainly never met me. I probably had a couple dozen half brothers and sisters too, maybe even here in Pelican View, and he was and he wasn't their father either.

Come to think of it, I hope they keep good records at the sperm donor clinic. Those half relatives will come in handy in the event that I need an organ donation someday.

A Day at the Farm

My story takes a decidedly dangerous turn on the morning of our visit to Happy Cattle Dairy Farm. Needless to say, I always position myself just in back of the bus driver to take advantage of the extra protection offered by the plastic barrier located behind her head. Originally intended to shield the bus driver from spitballs, it might hold the weight of my body in a minor impact situation.

Sitting up front also allows extra protection from the criminal activities of the Pelican View Basketball Team. Our teacher, Ms. Rita Linski, always sits in the first seat on the passenger side of Bus Number 987. This way, she can talk to the bus driver about her favorite subject: her collection of cereal box premiums, charms, and toys dating back to 1947.

Normally this would be a problem for me. I do not like to see the bus driver distracted in any way. On long bus rides, Ms. Linski even swings her knees into the aisle so that the bus driver can hear her stories better. While I do not recommend this posture—it is clearly in violation of the Pelican View School District's code of conduct—I'm willing to overlook the safety infraction, as this puts Ms. Linski in full view of any criminal activities that might involve me and the Pelican View Basketball Team.

Everything was going along as planned. Or so I thought. I

boarded the bus dead last in order to avoid being stepped on by members of the basketball team. Ms. Linski was supposed to follow directly, but something was detaining her. She seemed to be holding a very long conference with Mr. Putman, our school principal. Between them was someone else, someone rough and wild and unsanitary-looking. This someone else boarded the bus just behind Ms. Linski.

"Marvin, if you please, our agreement," Ms. Linski shouted to the back of the bus, shielding with her body the someone I was attempting to get a better look at.

Marvin Howerton was the captain of the basketball team. Ms. Linski was always making agreements with him. Basically, she insisted that he not get into trouble by messing up kids who were not on the basketball team, setting off fire alarms, or shaking up her six-packs of diet bubble gum soda. He agreed to whatever she said.

When will Ms. Linski learn? Marvin has a very short memory.

She followed Marvin with her eyes until he settled himself nearer the front. I lost all feeling in my fingers and my toes. I was now directly in his line of fire.

"Franklin, I would appreciate it if you would be Sarah's partner at the farm. She's just arrived at Pelican View, and we want to make her feel welcome." Sarah pressed around Ms. Linski to get a look at me. She put her hands on her hips and glanced back over her shoulder.

"You're joking," she said.

"I'll overlook that comment for your sake, Miss Kervick. Franklin, this is Sarah Kervick."

I'm sure my mouth just hung open. I'd never seen a finer host for parasites than the girl staring back at me. In less than thirty seconds, she would be sitting close enough for her fleas to change their address.

"Franklin, remember your manners."

"Yes, Ms. Linski," I said automatically.

"Don't bother, kid," said Sarah Kervick, flopping down on the seat as far away from me as the metal armrest would allow.

For this, I was truly thankful.

I tried not to stare at her. I felt frozen. Honest to Pete, my limbs would not move. I needed at least seven minutes to think through how I could protect myself from the thousands of germs that farm animals produce as well as the thousands that were already hovering around her.

I did have on my Gore-Tex jacket, the one that wicked perspiration away from my skin while shielding me from the bitter winds. This would provide some protection for my torso. I had hoped to bring a pair of the disposable sanitary gloves my grandparents had given me for my birthday, but my mother thought they would attract too much attention.

"You're gonna look like a white Michael Jackson," she said. "Only people with that kind of money can afford to be so weird."

This is the kind of love and support I get in my home environment.

On the bright side, Sarah Kervick's body would make it more difficult for Marvin to shoot projectiles at me.

She was not wearing a jacket at all, only a thin cardigan that had begun unraveling at the bottom. Underneath, she wore a cotton dress that ended above her bony knees. I noticed, too, that she had a wart on her knee.

But the most surprising thing about Sarah Kervick was her hair. It was all matted and messed up like she never combed it. Big, long pieces of dirty blond hair so tangled together it looked like there was a throw pillow crocheted onto the back of her head.

The bus lurched to a start. I covered my nose to keep from inhaling the diesel fumes.

"So you get any new cereal toys?" the bus driver asked predictably. Her name was Princess, and her driving record was far from clean. My intestines began arranging themselves into a bunny knot.

"It's funny you should mention it," began Ms. Linski. "Last night I was surfing eBay when I saw a Dick Tracy decoder ring from 1952."

"I remember Dick Tracy. He's the one with the big chin."

"Still in the cellophane," Ms. Linski said joyously.

"Hey, look, Donuthead has a new girlfriend," Marvin said.

I had a small impulse to jump out of my seat, point at Marvin, and say, "Look, everyone, it can speak." But since this would be putting my health in jeopardy, I kept quiet.

Sarah Kervick shot a look at me. "Donuthead? Is that you?"

I shrugged.

"Why'd he call you that?"

"Possibly because Donuthead is my name. It's very convenient for Marvin that I have a name that is also an insult," I answered her, keeping my voice low. "As a rule, he is not very creative."

"So whaddya do when he talks trash to you?"

"What do I do? Well, in a situation like this I would try to do as little as possible. It's important not to respond. That could escalate the tensions."

"You take his crap is what you're sayin'. Is that what you're sayin'?"

Sarah's voice had gotten both deeper and louder. Ms. Linski glanced over at us, but she did not stop talking.

"Yes, that is correct. I take it."

She folded her shoulders in toward herself and hunched down in her seat.

"Some kinda partner I get. I got some kinda luck," she muttered to herself.

It occurred to me that I might say the same thing about myself.

"So is this your first date, Donuthead? You takin' her to a cow farm?"

Sarah Kervick turned to face Marvin. "I give you one warning, kid."

"One warning for what? You think you and Donuthead can keep your love a secret?"

Then it happened. I can't give a very clear picture because I think I lost consciousness. I mean, my life passed before my eyes. There I was at five trying on the first bulletproof vest I'd begged my mother for when the lurching bus caused my head to crash into Princess's plastic protective shield.

Sarah Kervick had leapt over the armrest and smashed her fist into Marvin Howerton's nose. Blood was everywhere. Ms. Linski was screaming. Pandemonium broke loose.

Princess pulled over to the side of the road and tossed Ms. Linski a rag to press against Marvin's bloody face. Sarah had retreated to her seat, her arms folded across her chest. I saw with horror that she had Marvin's blood on the back of her fist and she didn't even seem to notice or care. Just moments ago, that very same blood was traveling around somewhere inside Marvin Howerton's nose.

"She broke it, Ms. Linski," Marvin howled. "She broke my nose."

Only it sounded more like "She bok by dobe" because Marvin's face was all folded up inside the oily rag.

"Now, Marvin, lean your head back," said Ms. Linski. "Sarah Kervick, is this the kind of girl you are?" she asked, shooting a look over her shoulder at Sarah. For the first time it seemed to dawn on our teacher that, probably, yes, girls who looked like Sarah Kervick were capable of committing bodily harm.

"I don't take crap from anybody," Sarah Kervick replied. "We might as well get that straight right now."

Needless to say, I did not escort Sarah Kervick around Happy Cattle Dairy Farm.

She remained on the bus while I was forced to slog through the melting snow and cow pies on my own, since everyone else had already been paired off. I was so preoccupied by thoughts of what had happened that I let a cow lick my palm!

When I asked about the facilities so I could wash my hands, Ms. Linski pointed to one of those mobile metal waste containment units, otherwise known as a Porta-John. I held my hand away from the rest of my body until we were back at school. I had quite a cramp by the time we reached Pelican View Elementary.

The bus was strangely quiet on the way back. Ms. Linski sat with her lips pressed together. Sarah Kervick leaned forward in her seat, staring at a piece of petrified gum on the floor of the bus. Marvin, who was beginning to bruise beneath both eyes, moaned a little now and then and shot threatening looks at me!

What had I done but try *not* to escalate tensions?

Then it occurred to me that Sarah Kervick had punched Marvin in the nose, at least partly, on my account. I got a strange feeling then. No one had ever stuck up for Franklin Delano Donuthead before.

Not that I blamed them. I would never attempt to come between a bully and his victim. To do so would put me at a disproportionately high risk of injuring my cranio-facial muscles.

In fact, it is a strong evolutionary trait to want to avoid people like Marvin Howerton. Take those nature programs on TV—the ones where the lioness goes off to find dinner—and you'll know what I mean. She slinks along, tracking a herd of innocent gazelles who are just minding their own business on the Serengeti Plain. Crouching, she finds a victim: a baby or a weakling or maybe just a highly intelligent yet slightly handicapped gazelle. And off she goes.

What do this poor gazelle's lifelong companions do? Do they rally the troops? Do they shout "Safety in numbers!" and smother that lioness before she can harm one of their own? Of course they don't. They run just as fast as they can away from the scene of the crime, not even pausing to nod a fond farewell.

After all, they don't want to be dessert. And that's the way it is at school.

I looked up and down the rows of kids jiggling in their bus seats, searching for one person who might brave a darkened corner of the playground to save my life from Marvin Howerton. Not one came to mind. They'd run, just like the gazelles.

That's nature for you.

Sarah Kervick stole a look at me just as Princess hopped the curb as she turned into Pelican View Elementary School.

"What's the matter, kid? How come your arm's stickin' out like that?"

"A cow licked my palm."

"You're joking, right?"

I nodded my head soberly. "Only a foolish optimist can deny the dark realities of the moment," I said.

"Huh?"

"That's what Franklin Delano Roosevelt said when he took office during the Depression."

Sarah Kervick laughed, revealing a couple of brown teeth.

"That where you get your information? Dead presidents?"

At least it was a real laugh and not one of those hee-hee girl giggles that means a girl's really making fun of you. I believe she actually thought I was funny.

It was also a laugh that could not come out of any sane person who saw the trouble that lay ahead.

"Marvin, Sarah, come with me. The rest of you may return to class and start your journals."

I was first off the bus after Marvin and Sarah, and I watched them as long as I could. She went first. I wanted, somehow, to tell her never, ever offer your back to Marvin Howerton. But she didn't seem to care.

I was so busy thinking about all this that I walked right by the boys' bathroom and straight to class. That meant I'd be forced to infect my pencil with mad cow germs until Ms. Linski gave me a hall pass. How long could they possibly live in the arid environment of a number 2B pencil?

To calm myself, I began to hum the tune to the "Happy Birthday" song, an exercise I repeated three times while lathering whenever I washed my hands. Just as I reached my last "to you," however, my thoughts bounced back to bony old Sarah Kervick.

Had that girl ever been introduced to a comb? What kind of a mother would let her child leave the house in such a condition? Was she really laughing at what I said? Or was she just laughing at me?

Was this what Gloria had in mind when she told me to think more about girls?

CHAPTER THREE

The "Out Back" Beauty School

Two days later, I sat at the kitchen table eating my bowl of Bran Buds and editing my mother's grocery list, which she had tried to conceal under yesterday's newspaper. I had already crossed off some questionable choices as well as added a few items of my own when she arrived on the scene and rudely grabbed the paper away from me.

"How'd you get ahold of that?" she asked, attaching her Cable Country name badge between the second and third buttons on her blouse. My mother lays cable for a company whose motto is "Get wired!"

"For your information, Franklin, millions of people eat these things every day. What could possibly be wrong with . . . jellybeans?"

"The connection between artificial dyes and children's behavior is currently being studied by public health officials."

"So don't eat any. Hot dogs? Oreos?"

"Nitrates and hydrogenated vegetable oil. Do you really want to feed your only son, the one you hope to care for you in old age, a diet full of known cancer-causing agents?"

"Let me think about that one," she said, putting the list on the counter and scooping handfuls of beans into the coffee grinder.

"Pepper spray? You mean the kind . . ." She perused the rest of the list, folded it, and put it into her pocket.

"Mace? Funeral plots? Franklin?"

"I think it's only right that you should know," I told her, my eyelids twitching. "Things are really heating up at school."

"All this because you got licked by a cow?"

I wish.

No, the cow contamination incident was the furthest thing from my mind. For you see, something far stranger and more perilous happened the day after our visit to Happy Cattle Dairy Farm.

Ms. Linski decided, for some reason fathomable only to high priestesses in India, that I would be a stabilizing influence on Sarah Kervick.

"Sarah will sit next to you, Franklin. And if she needs help, you will provide her with it. Quietly."

Mentally, I calculated the effects of Ms. Linski's words on my health. "Quietly" meant whispering. Whispering meant closeness. Closeness meant contamination range. Every time I thought of Sarah Kervick's mouth and hair coming into contact with my breathing space, my blood pressure inched toward the ceiling.

But it seemed that Sarah Kervick did not want to ask me anything. She spent most of the morning leaning back in her seat with her hands pushed up under her armpits as if she were unbearably cold. When Ms. Linski asked Sarah to open her math book, she simply raised one eyebrow and flipped the book over.

Something told me Sarah Kervick was not National Merit Scholar material.

After lunch, I came back to find a note on my desk. It said, "Met me tomorow after scool. Owt bak."

I glanced over at Sarah Kervick. A torn sheet of paper and a pencil had replaced the overturned math book.

"I'm afraid that's impossible," I said, keeping my voice low. "I'm having my left hamstring professionally stretched tomorrow. You see, one of my legs—"

"You be there," she returned, in what could be interpreted as a growl.

"These appointments are very hard to get," I told her, searching my mind for the made-up name of an impressive-sounding doctor.

"Because I'm gonna wrap your tongue around your neck and choke you with it if you don't come."

"I see. Well." There didn't seem to be any more to say on the subject.

"Could you add psychological counseling to that list?" I now asked my mother as she filled a quart-size thermos with coffee.

"I can't afford counseling for you! If anybody needs counseling around here, it's me! I go to work every day and run errands on my lunch hour. Try to go to the grocery store and live in the same house with a kid like you! The produce is covered with pesticides, the cookies are filled with oxygenated vegetable oil—"

"That's hydrogenated."

". . . the hot dogs are poison, the jellybeans are diseased—"

"I never said they were diseased!"

"Funeral plots!"

"Well, if you must know, I've been invited to meet the most fearsome student in Ms. Rita Linski's fifth-grade class after school *behind* the school," I shouted back in defense. "This is not where the buses pick up, Mother. They do not mow this part of the property! There are glass shards, cigarette butts, possibly even human remains back there!"

My mother walked over and cupped my chin, turning my head this way and that. "I think Grandma was right," she said, finally. "You need something to distract you from all these crazy fantasies about shrinking and contamination and violence."

She went over to the counter, picked up a knife, and stabbed it into a tub of room-temperature margarine.

As she slathered her toast, she said, "You need what every red-blooded American boy needs, Franklin, and that is baseball."

A nerve beneath my left eye began pulsing wildly.

"How you can mention blood and baseball in the same sentence while I am attempting to ward off an anxiety attack about a far more immediate issue of danger is beyond me," I managed to choke out.

"Marvin Howerton, then," my mother said, snapping on her tool belt. "Is that what this is about? Marvin Howerton?"

I simply looked at her with tear-filled eyes. I was letting her imagination do the rest. The name Sarah Kervick could not possibly have conjured up the same horrible image as the one of her son flat on his back with Marvin Howerton's beefy fists dangling over him.

My mother stared at me. Then she shoved a triangle of toast into her mouth.

"Remember to lead with your long arm," she said, and she was gone.

How I have survived to this day, I cannot tell you.

At school, I experienced a feeling close to rapture when I realized that Sarah Kervick was absent! I gazed lovingly at the empty seat of her desk until the thought occurred to me that she might be at home twisting rope into a coil or lifting weights in anticipation of our after-school meeting.

Never has a school day gone by so fast. Never have I felt so sentimental about multiplying fractions or westward expansion or even Ms. Linski's cereal box premium collection.

I was so distracted I forgot to check the surface of my seat upon returning from the pencil sharpener. I sat directly on a piece of gum that had been masticated by none other than Marvin Howerton. Though I immediately applied liquid Goo Gone from the travel bottle I keep in my desk, it made me feel slightly nauseated for the rest of the day to think that Marvin Howerton's saliva had made contact with my clothes.

At 3:15, I tried to engage Ms. Linski in a long discussion on the merits of decoder rings over, say, two-way wristband radios. But she was not interested.

"It's time to pack up, Franklin," she said, flinging our carefully researched papers into her schoolbag and dismissing me without a backward look.

This roller coaster of emotion was definitely not good for my health. I decided to take my blood pressure with the sphygmomanometer my grandparents had given me for Christmas as soon as I got home.

As I collected my things, I reasoned that it was entirely possible that Sarah Kervick had fallen victim to some tragic domestic accident and would be unable to make our meeting. Most accidental deaths occur within five miles of one's home.

What was I thinking? I was less than five miles from home myself. As Ms. Linski waited, clucking in the doorway, I weighed my options. Break for home was the odds-on favorite, but it didn't look so good as a long-range plan. I had a feeling that a make-up session with Sarah Kervick would be even more dangerous than what was in store for me today. So, I decided to simply peek around the corner on my way to the safety-assisted crosswalk to assure myself that the meeting was, indeed, off.

This being March, there was no tall grass to keep me from seeing her, hunkered down on the sidewalk, waiting for me at the opposite end of the basketball courts. Her bony knees stuck out from her dress like two flamingo legs. When Sarah Kervick saw me, she motioned me over with her thumb.

Hobbling across the pavement toward her, I felt a growing numbness in my legs. As I gazed at the naked trees, the basketball hoops, the four square on the asphalt, it all seemed unbearably beautiful.

"O Precious World," I cried, and sank to my knees.

Within seconds, Sarah Kervick was hauling me up by my jacket lapels and dragging me bodily to a deserted corner of the schoolyard. Judging by the amount of discarded cigarette packs and candy bar wrappers, I realized that what I'd told my mother was true. Even the janitor, Mr. Shorevitz, never came back here.

Now I understood how doomed mobsters felt when being "taken for a drive."

Sarah Kervick stood me on my feet and raised her arm. I noticed something in her right hand, glinting in the sun. I stared at it, transfixed, waiting for life to end. It took me a moment to realize this was not high-carbon stainless steel. This was . . . plastic. Tortoiseshell, to be exact. This was a comb.

"Comb it," she growled.

"Comb it," I repeated, frozen to the spot.

"And if I ever hear you told, I'll use this comb to brush your teeth and make you gargle with chlorine bleach."

She slapped the comb in my palm, turned around, and folded her arms.

Despite myself, I almost blurted it out: *Why me? Do I look like a kid who would know something about this kind of female activity?*

But a life has to be lived on principle. I would not be swayed from my principles, even in the heat of the moment. And the most important principle was, *Do not escalate tensions!*

I pinched a mass of dirty, matted hair between my fingers and felt like the miller's daughter, the one who was supposed to spin straw into gold. Now that my life did not seem in immediate danger, I began to calculate the probability of contracting head lice from this exercise.

"Go on. Pull hard! You can't hurt me." Sarah Kervick took all the ratty, stringy hairs from underneath her sweater and flattened them down against her back.

For a second time I was tempted to incite her to violence by asking why she didn't just do the job herself. I had barely begun when the answer revealed itself. Her hair was so knotted that there was no way to separate one side from the other. She'd have to be a contortionist to complete the project by herself. I began by applying the comb to the most promising section of hair, the bottom half inch. Instantly, I met resistance. I tugged. I believe I saw her wince. Was it possible that Sarah Kervick felt pain? And where was my anti-bacterial, sanitizing hand wash—the kind you use without water—when I needed it?

I worked until I lost all feeling in my toes from the cold. Picturing the blackened lumps inside my shoes, I almost got up the courage to ask her if we could at least go back to my house, where yes! we enjoyed the modern convenience of an efficient gas heater with a dust and mold filter.

But then I had to weigh losing a few toes against the knowledge that Sarah Kervick knew where I lived.

"Franklin?"

A shadowy figure in the distance caught my eye and began to take form. Never had I been so happy, so utterly delighted, to see my mother! And she was wearing her tool belt, which clanked as she walked toward us and made her look rather menacing, I can tell you.

"Who are you?" Sarah Kervick asked.

I waited for my mother to dress her down. Show me a woman who could stand up to Sarah Kervick and I'll show you my mother, I thought. I swear the national anthem started playing in my head.

"I'm Franklin's mother," she said, more surprised than angry. "And I came here to pick up the pieces of my son I imagined were strewn all over the playground."

"Huh," Sarah Kervick huffed. "Some imagination."

Mother took it all in: the knotted tangles of Sarah Kervick's hair, the comb in my hand. Gently, she took Sarah by the shoulders and turned her around.

"For this, you will need a detangler, dear."

Dear!

"I think I've got some at home. Do you want to try it?"

Sarah pulled a hunk of hair off her shoulder and examined it. She looked at me, disgusted. Then she shrugged her shoulders.

"Why not?" she said. And she followed my mother—a complete stranger to her!—right into the van.

They left me standing on the playground with my mouth open, comb in hand.

This truly is a world of wonders.

CHAPTER FOUR

A Life of Crime

Sarah Kervick was very interested in my mother's van. She pressed the window button a couple of times and let her hands travel back and forth along the seat until she saw me watching her. Then she stopped and looked out the window.

"I'm Julia, by the way," my mother said after she turned the volume on the radio down.

"Oh, hi," Sarah said, all shy.

"And you are . . ."

"Sarah Kervick," I told her.

"Sarah," she repeated after me. "Just Sarah."

It wasn't far to our house. As we turned into the driveway, I saw it the way Sarah Kervick might have, just another boxy brick ranch built in the 1950s to withstand a nuclear explosion. It rose out of the center of a ring of vegetation that threatened to swallow it up. In late spring or summer or even fall, our yard is filled with flowers and flowering bushes and trees. My mother is a little obsessive about flowers.

And since she's careful not to breed allergy-inducing plants, I can enjoy them, too. Except the strongly scented ones. Or lilies with stamens that stain your clothes. Or bee-attracting varieties. Allergic reactions to bee stings have caused the untimely death of many a child.

But just now, in mid-March, the dried puffs of hydrangea

blossoms lay beaten at the edge of the lawn, and the ferns looked as if someone had singed them with a blowtorch, their fronds all brown and crackled on the ground. The grassy areas were respectable enough, except where my mother and I had worn them away, she forcing me to engage in that medieval event otherwise known as batting practice and me jumping to get out of the way of her pitches.

"I like this house," Sarah said under her breath as we pulled into the driveway. "But who's he?"

I followed her finger to Bernie Lepner, who was currently tucked away under one of our yew bushes.

My mother calls Bernie "dreamy." He's in fourth grade, and his favorite game is still make-believe. And his favorite place to make believe is in the bushes around our house. You see, Bernie's parents are more traditional. They favor the lollipop-bush style of landscaping. Their yard is tidy and sanitary and unlikely to attract vermin. But it doesn't lend itself well to make-believe.

"Hey, Bern," my mother said as she jumped out of the van. "What's going on in Rebeltown?"

Rebeltown is the name of the kingdom Bernie has created under our front porch.

"Hi, Julia," Bernie said, smiling up at her from under a cloud of bangs. "There's a porcupine stampede going on right now."

"This is our friend Sarah," my mother said. Bernie gave Sarah a smile, too, as she and my mother bent closer to see the action. He'd scattered the prickly poppy husks from last summer across the ground beneath the yew bush. They were his porcupines.

I wasn't so interested in this because it was one of Bernie's favorite episodes and he replayed it several times a month.

"Franklin, I got another name for our list."

"That's fine," I said. "We can talk about it *later* . . ."

"Stuart Little. He has a boating accident," Bernie replied, flicking over some porcupine casualties with his finger and ignoring my request.

"So he does."

"And a terrible leak in his birch-bark canoe, so that's two water accidents."

"Yeah, okay. Well, we've got work to do here," I said, backing up the front steps, hoping Bernie would get the hint.

"And he gets rolled up in a window shade, but I wasn't sure how to classify that."

Sarah Kervick had picked up one of Bernie's porcupines and was stroking it with her finger.

"What's he talkin' about?" she asked.

"Bernie and Franklin have this list of characters in literature who are most likely to die in a preventable accident," my mother said, wiping the dirt off her hands and standing up. "It's something they do for fun."

"We already got Pippi Longstocking, Tom Sawyer, the Hardy Boys, Peter from *Heidi*, Jack the Giant Killer, and Ralph the Motorcycle Mouse, but we haven't ranked them yet," Bernie said in a rush. "We're trying to decide if we should make two lists, one for the kids and one for the animals."

I made a mental note never to share any classified information with Bernie.

Sarah Kervick stood up and carefully replaced Bernie's

porcupine. Wiping her hands on her dress, she headed up the steps with my mother. "Some fun," she said.

Bernie went back to his porcupine battle plan. What else could I do but follow my mother and Sarah Kervick?

Normally, after school, my mother and I debrief at the kitchen counter. She tells me the joke that her boss pastes on the watercooler while I wash my hands. Then I slice up some organic fruit and muesli, and she eats one of those prepackaged snacks filled with artificial dyes and preservatives.

"Want a Twinkie?" she asked Sarah, pressing me up against the lip of the sink in her haste to get to the pantry.

"Sure," Sarah said. I'd never seen her so agreeable.

I tried once again to lather up my hands, but my mother jostled past me for a second time, disturbing my concentration. I'd been humming the "Happy Birthday" song under my breath, and her body blocks made me lose my place.

"Chocolate milk?"

"Do you have some?" The way Sarah Kervick asked, with such astonishment, it was as if she'd never seen chocolate milk and Twinkies in the same place before.

While it seemed irresponsible for my mother to lead Sarah Kervick down the road to nutritional ruin, I wasn't about to say so. I waited for her to raid the refrigerator once again before I reached in and pulled out an organic apple.

"So, how'd it get this way? Your hair?" my mother asked after they'd settled at the kitchen table.

Sarah Kervick picked up her Twinkie and put it down again. She shrugged her shoulders.

"Fair enough." My mother grabbed a paper napkin from the

pile in the middle of the table. "Sometimes things just get away from you. Now you get to ask me a question."

Sarah smiled a little smile to herself and looked down at her plate. She took a wolf-size bite from her Twinkie, just sort of snapped it in two, and said through the food, "So it's just you and him that live here?"

My mother returned the smile. "Just me and him," she said. Then she leaned forward on her elbows and lowered her voice. "You wouldn't think so to look at him, but Franklin takes up quite a bit of space."

That made Sarah laugh, and my mother sat back, satisfied, and took the same-size bite out of her Twinkie.

I decided to forgo the muesli and take my apple to my room. After all, they hadn't even waited for me to reach the table to begin eating.

My room is my sanctuary. No one is allowed in here. Certainly not my mother, whose boots have been in unseemly places and probably carry boatloads of bacteria on each sole. Every evening before I go to bed, I vacuum my carpet in an east-west pattern that never fails to show the footprints of intruders. Twice I've caught my mother, who claimed to be looking for her car keys. Bernie has tried, too. Even the dog, Baron, before his untimely demise, breached security when my mother invited him in for half a ham sandwich.

Everything in my room is neatly organized, categorized, and sterilized. My Lego kits are fully assembled and covered with the kind of protective plastic used in the dry-cleaning industry. The sheets over my bookcases protect the pages from dust spores as well as damaging ultraviolet rays, and my diagnostic medical equipment is stored in a locked filing cabinet. Surge protectors and antivirus software keep my computer in good working order. When not in use, it is covered with a heavy anti-static nylon cover. Having said all this, I think it's quite plain that havoc could be wreaked if visitors were allowed in here.

After measuring my arms and legs and noting the slight variations from yesterday in my notebook, I sat on my bed and thought about what to do.

Should I eat my apple slowly, to aid in digestion? Should I add Stuart Little to my database? Should I read another chapter of *Diet for a Poisoned Planet*?

I walked to the entrance of my room and poked my head into the hall, where I heard the sound of laughter and talk floating down from the kitchen.

"Why's he do a thing like that?" Sarah said.

"Hold still. This might hurt a little," my mother replied. "He thinks his arms and legs are two different sizes. Am I pulling too hard?"

"Go on and pull. You can't hurt me."

There was a long silence, during which I imagined Sarah Kervick in serious pain.

"Are they?" she asked, kind of grunting it out, as if through clenched teeth.

"Sorry. What?"

"Are they different sizes? His legs?"

"Oh. They might as well be. Franklin looks so hard for what's wrong with him, he's bound to turn up something."

I went back inside my room and closed the door. At this stage of my life it might be nice to have a decent friend, I thought, mentally crossing my mother off the list. Someone tidy like myself, someone who understood a *sensitive* young man. At the very least, perhaps I could have a mother who took my physical abnormalities seriously and who realized that not all boys were meant to play third base for the New York Yankees, even though their blood was indeed red.

Take Hans Christian Andersen, for example. He had the widow Bunkeflod to listen sympathetically when he poured out his troubles. *She* understood his little idiosyncrasies, like the languages he made up that no one could understand, and his need to stuff pamphlets into his clothes to make himself look bigger. Without her sympathy, we might never have had "The Ugly Duckling," or "The Little Mermaid," or "The Steadfast Tin Soldier."

Myself, I would prefer someone a little younger, with all her own teeth and no dowager's hump. I'd been thinking very seriously about what Gloria said, but it never went anywhere. There *was* a certain someone at school who had caught my eye, but I didn't have a shred of evidence that I'd caught hers.

I don't know what it was. As I sat there on the edge of my bed, I felt paralyzed with this sadness. All of a sudden, it hit me that there might not be a person on this earth who would ever appreciate me.

I guess you could say my mother has hidden talents. I mean, her only child is a boy. Where did she learn to comb out girl hair? By the time I felt it safe to venture back to the kitchen, she was finished. I expected Sarah to be bald. But she wasn't. Her hair looked okay. Even something close to clean.

"Do you need a ride home?" my mother asked Sarah.

"No, that's okay. I can walk."

To where? I wondered, having trouble imagining a boxy brick house that contained Sarah Kervick and her mom and dad and all their ratty, unraveling sweaters.

"Come back tomorrow and I'll give you some cream rinse to help keep it smooth," my mother said. "You can walk home with Franklin."

As she passed by us on her way out the door, Sarah glared at me as if that were the last thing she wanted to do.

Well, excuse me.

I watched her go, all the way down the block. When she thought she was a safe distance from the house, she started skipping. Then, on the corner, she stopped, letting her hands travel up and down the back of her head. When she started skipping again, she proceeded directly into the street. Without even looking both ways.

My mother moved to Pelican View so that I would have a safe place to grow up. Maybe I should be thankful she didn't want to live on the Lower East Side of New York City or Calcutta, India, but frankly, it was hard to feel grateful the following day when I found myself walking home with Sarah Kervick.

We headed home along Main Street, past Fortuna's Hobby Shop, the post office, and Professor Quiggle's Book Nook. Sarah walked about six steps ahead, which was just fine with me. Being seen with her wasn't exactly good for my reputation, either.

Suddenly, she stopped dead in front of Perkins' Drug

Store. As I came up behind her, I could see she was staring at a picture of a lady holding out her hands in front of her and smiling.

"No more unsightly warts!" the lady announced to the camera. "Finally, I can go out again."

I continued on my way, past a frozen Sarah Kervick. Suddenly, her hand shot out, grabbed me by the shoulder in some kind of kung-fu torture grip, and twirled me around.

"Listen," she said. "I want some of that stuff."

I remembered the wart on her knee. But now, with her hand on my shoulder, I saw something else. She had warts on her fingers, too. Notice I said *warts*, as in plural. Let's just say more warts than most ladies have rings.

"Fine," I said, trying to sound calm as I imagined wart juices leaking onto my jacket. "I'll wait here."

"Not me. You go in there and get some."

"I'd be happy to buy you some wart remover. Really, I would do it gladly," I replied in the same tone of voice I might use when talking to a malnourished Bengal tiger. "But I don't have any money right now."

"No problem there," said Sarah, pointing to an emblem on the front door. "They take MasterCard and Visa."

"But I don't—"

"Listen, punk," she whispered, moving her hand from my shoulder to my throat. Her fingers were now inside my jacket, close to the skin. She had penetrated my first line of defense! Now seemed a good time to panic.

"You may like being a freak. You may get something out of it. But I don't. Now go in there and get me some of that stuff in the picture. Do it any way you know how. Do it or I'm going to push on these shoulders"—with her hands, she demonstrated some sort of crushing Slavic nutcracker technique that would result in one's lungs exchanging places—"until I close you like a suitcase."

As soon as I finished hyperventilating, I straightened my jacket and entered the store. Perkins' was an old-fashioned drugstore with a soda fountain up front and the shop in the back. Mr. Perkins is the third Mr. Perkins to run this store. He is always impeccably dressed, with a red bow tie peeking out of a starched white lab coat. While his personal cleanliness is not to be questioned, we have had many conversations regarding public health and food-borne illnesses.

As a rule, you see, I refuse to eat in a restaurant. I know what those service people are doing behind the swinging double doors. Once, I caught sight of a greasy-haired teenager dragging my glass through the ice machine without gloves on! Unfortunately, I had to report him to the health inspector right away. Mr. Perkins was very sorry to hear about that.

"Oh, hello, Franklin." Mr. Perkins smiled at me. "I'll be with you in a minute." And he went in the back, like he always did, to get the results of his most recent health inspection.

I realized that this was my moment. My moment! With Mr. Perkins off the floor, I could accomplish my dirty deed and be gone. How unprepared I was. Where were the wart removers? In Beauty Aids? In Topical Applications? As I frantically raced up and down the aisles, Mr. Perkins reappeared with a handful of papers.

"I'm so sorry, Mr. Perkins," I said, panting. "I don't want

anything to eat. I was just wondering . . . er . . . do you have any wart remover?"

"Oh. Sure. In Foot Care. What kind of wart is it?"

I realized with horror that he thought I, Franklin Delano Donuthead, was the carrier of a fungal virus.

"Fortunately, I am disease-free, Mr. Perkins. It's my . . . my mother who suffers."

"Oh, okay. Where's the wart?"

"The wart is on her . . ." I glanced between the blinds to see that Sarah Kervick had not deserted her post. Her hands were shoved up under her armpits, and she was leaning against the mailbox, frowning. Poor old Mrs. Finster, who at ninety-seven was the oldest lady in town, was trying to straighten up long enough to mail a letter.

"Her finger," I said, finally.

"And is it raised or below the surface of the skin?"

"I would say . . . raised."

I followed Mr. Perkins's crisp white lab coat through the aisles to the Foot Care section, where every manner of disgusting and horrifying condition was depicted on the packages. Treatments for warts, corns, athlete's foot, and excessive odor lined the shelves.

"She has a couple of options, Franklin. She can use this solution and paint it on with a brush . . . sort of like fingernail polish," he said, smiling at me as if we men understood something about the way women like to do things.

"Or she can use this specially treated bandage approach for several days. Or, what I recommend most often, because it's economical, is this patch. You can cut it to the size of the wart and stick it on. But you should cover it with a regular bandage."

At that, Mr. Perkins left me to consider my choices. Little did he know that instead of weighing my choices of various topical treatments, I was envisioning a long prison term, eating food laced with lard, and bathing *barefoot* in a public shower with men who had committed violent crimes.

Hands shaking, I reached for the most economical choice. Maybe I could get my sentence reduced by pleading that I was trying to have as little effect on Mr. Perkins's financial picture as possible. As I started to stuff the sheet of acid-coated paper into my jacket pocket, I froze.

Seeing my distorted reflection in the little round security mirror, I realized I was standing at a crossroads in my life. Not just the intersection between Foot Care and Beauty Aids but a point where I had to choose between doing the honorable thing and doing the cowardly thing. It was the point in the story . . . *my* story, mind you, where the hero's character is tested. Yes, this was a character-building moment!

I decided to throw myself on the mercy of the pharmacist.

"Mr. Perkins," I called, jogging through the store until I found him in Seasonal Items. "Have you ever had the opportunity to steer some down-on-his-luck youngster away from a life of crime?"

Mr. Perkins thought about that for a moment. "Well, Franklin, I would have to say yes to that. You'd be surprised at the number of children who come in here and take things without paying."

"Well, I for one will not swell their ranks, Mr. Perkins," I declared, slapping the wart treatment on the counter.

And I told him my story.

When I was finished, Mr. Perkins walked casually over to the front window and began to straighten the greeting cards. As he was doing that, he glanced outside. Then he came strolling back to me.

"Franklin," he said. "I'll tell you what. I have a fund for situations like this one. I'll give you what you need and the fund will take care of paying for it. And this will remain just between you and me, Franklin."

"Mr. Perkins," I said solemnly. "Someday, when I occupy a highly respected position in the community, I will repay you for this kindness."

And I reached out to shake his hand, which I think he knew well was a gesture of my greatest respect. Mr. Perkins went back to Foot Care and put two more sheets of wart paper into a small bag. Then he went to First Aid and added a tin of bandages and a manicure scissors.

I walked out of the store with my head held high and handed over the bag. Sarah grabbed it without saying thank you and squinted furiously at the glass window of Perkins' Drug Store.

"You were holdin' out on me," she said.

"I beg your pardon?"

"Most times, when you lift something, they don't give you a bag."

As I stared at the bag, the thought occurred to me that maybe Sarah Kervick was not as violent as she first appeared.

Maybe she was like one of those wolf girls, raised in a cave in India and later found by missionaries. She just had no understanding of the rules of polite society. Besides, she could hardly grind me into a pulp right here on Main Street in front of Perkins' Drug Store.

"When I undertake a project, Miss Kervick," I said, straightening the lapels of my jacket, "I always do it with a touch of class."

At that she laughed, throwing her head back and looking directly at the sun. Then she continued walking six steps in front of me to my house. Which is very strange, considering I never gave her the directions. And she'd only been there once.

"Tell me something," she said after a fourteen-block silence. "This freaky stuff you got goin' about germs and all. Is that a act?"

We rounded the corner and crossed the street to my block. The wind had picked up, and I dug my hands deeper into my pockets, hunching forward.

"If you're referring to the attention I pay to my personal hygiene, I assure you I am completely in earnest."

"So it's for real?" She stopped, waiting for me to catch up. When I was as close as I was likely to get, Sarah Kervick asked me, "Does a kid like you have any friends?"

For a moment we faced each other in silence, shivering there in the cold. I'd never really looked at it that way before. I mean, I have always felt that when the right candidate came along, we would be fast friends. Trouble was, there were *no* candidates, let alone right ones. The kids at Pelican View Elementary weren't exactly vying for the honor of hanging out with Franklin Delano Donuthead.

I started to feel this sadness again, creeping up under my shirt and wrapping my heart in cold Styrofoam. I thumped my chest, wishing Sarah Kervick would stop looking at me, wishing I could, just for once, not be the object of someone's pity.

"Do you ever watch those nature programs where the lioness goes after the herd of gazelles?" I asked her, blowing into my hands as if, somehow, miraculously, this would ease the icy feeling in my chest.

"Sure. I like that stuff."

"Well," I said, "I have a theory about that."

And so I told her my theory of the weakest gazelle and the elementary school playground. She nodded in agreement. You can't attend elementary school and not see the truth in this comparison.

When I finished, Sarah Kervick lifted one eyebrow and slapped me on the back. I lost my balance and stumbled dangerously close to the curb.

"You're a smart kid, Donuthead," she said. "You got a lotta fancy theories. But I think you need to know something about the playground."

She looked off into the distance, trying to figure out how to explain herself to me. It was then I noticed. Her lips were blue. It was cold! Her fingers and her kneecaps were red and chapped. But if Sarah Kervick felt any pain as a result of the weather, she wasn't letting on.

"You don't fight back, you get flattened. See, all the other kids, even the runts, will be lookin' to build their reputation on your back."

Sarah Kervick squared my shoulders and waited for me to meet her gaze.

"You gotta learn to fight, Donuthead."

By this time, my teeth were chattering. "Have you ever seen a gazelle win a standoff with a lion?"

She thought for a while. "No, but gazelles don't know the ground-floor punch, either."

"Ground-floor punch?" I repeated. Just talking about the possibility of violence was increasing my pulse rate. I lowered my head and pushed on, knowing my house wasn't far, and feeling right then the way an old horse feels about his stall in the barn.

She followed, closer than she normally did, kicking through the soggy piles of oak leaves at our feet and spattering mud on my shoes.

"When you're goin' after someone bigger, it's gotta be a surprise or it doesn't work."

Suddenly, she stopped. "Okay," she said, grabbing my shoulders and kicking my feet into a wider stance. "Put your feet like this. That's your power. Don't back down! Think you're Joe Louis or somethin'."

I studied Sarah Kervick for a minute. She really thought she was being helpful. She really thought that there was some possibility I would warm to the idea of perpetrating physical violence on another person. Not to mention that after one ineffective swing, that other person would be perpetrating physical violence on me.

"There is no such thing as security for any nation—or any individual—in a world ruled by the principles of gangsterism," I told her. "That quote was made possible by the late, great Franklin Delano Roosevelt. My namesake, I might add. I think I will follow his guidance, if you don't mind, Miss Kervick."

Sarah Kervick sighed. "You are one weird cluck, Donuthead," she said. "I was just sayin' you get it up in your face all the time because you don't fight back, that's all. I was tryin' to help you, kid."

Then she left me, standing on the sidewalk at the edge of my driveway, trying to bring myself to say thanks.

In the house, my mother was ready for us. She even had a snack waiting! Sarah sat on the barstool and politely ate four brownies and drank a container of orange juice. When Mother offered her another, she asked if she could save it for later. Another four brownies, three apples, and two boxes of juice went into a lunch bag.

Then my mother set a shopping bag on the table and pulled out a flower-print bag that looked like a miniature suitcase. She undid the two snaps just below the handles, and the bag opened flat on the table. Inside were two big, clear pockets. Stuffed in those pockets were enough toiletries to take a trip to the Far East and back. Shampoo, conditioner, hairbrush, soap, deodorant, toothpaste, toothbrush, you name it. Then there was a bunch of items I had trouble identifying, like complicated devices for sticking in hair and pots of questionable goo to make lips shiny.

Sarah and I just stared and stared. She wiped her mouth with the paper towel my mother had given her and reached over and closed the bag and snapped it and took hold of the handles.

"Where do you get a thing like this?" she asked, as if she were holding up a magic crystal ball and not a toiletry bag with a little tag that read "Made in China" on it.

"I got it at Selvidges, in the mall," my mother said. She was smiling. I could see she was really pleased.

Later, after Sarah left, with her toiletries and her bag from Perkins' in one hand and a bag with half our pantry in the other, I decided to have a talk with my mother.

"Why is it that when a stranger tries to manhandle your son, you give her presents?" I asked. "And when your son gives you a simple request, for, say, a can of Mace so he can protect himself against the evils of the world, you refuse?"

"I help her, Franklin . . . ," she responded, energetically sweeping crumbs off the counter into her palm. "No, let me put it this way. I *enjoy* helping Sarah Kervick . . ." She paused, dusting her hands off in the sink and returning to the counter to stare into my eyes. ". . . because she has real problems."

CHAPTER FIVE

I See Patterns

Some people take pills when they feel anxious. I review statistics. Statistics can be very calming. If you're caught in the middle of a thunderstorm, for example, and you're worried that you might be struck by lightning, it is comforting to know that according to the National Safety Department, your chances are about 2,794,493 to 1 of getting fried. Of course, this rises dramatically if you live in Singapore. Don't ask me why, but Singapore is the lightning capital of the world. It also rises if you live in Florida and like to golf a lot. A preference for metal clubs will not aid your profile, either. But for the most part, your chances of being struck by lightning in any given year are so small that you can confidently get home without a panic attack.

Sometimes, if I hear strange noises at night and am having trouble sleeping, I calculate the probability of a violent crime occurring at our address on that particular evening. To do this I take the number of days we have lived crime-free in the house, factor in the part of town in which we live and the absence of convictions on drug or fencing charges for the house's occupants (my mother and me), and come to the conclusion that it is highly unlikely anything life threatening will happen to us before daybreak.

So, all in all, statistics have always been my friend. My friendly guide, so to speak.

That is, until I came across a statistic that did not comfort me at all.

It happened not long after my mother became Sarah Kervick's hairdresser. I was innocently surfing the Web to find out more about seasonal patterns of deer-car collisions when I discovered that there is a factor that is more important to your health than what you eat or how much alcohol you drink or even having arms and legs that are different lengths. If you have this one thing, you can get through just about any catastrophic accident or illness and live out your normal life span. Even live longer than you are supposed to!

That one thing is hard to describe statistically. It's love, if you can believe that. The love of friends, of spouses, of neighbors, of teachers, of mothers who pester you to play ball with them, of dreamy little fourth graders who live next door and let their dogs wander the streets.

Put another way, there is an overwhelming amount of evidence to indicate that people who are socially isolated—that means they don't have friends or family—are two to five times more likely to die a premature death from all causes. Shocking!

Since the possibility of adding a father in the near future was not so good, and my mother's parents lived far away— they spend most of their time golfing (yes!) in Florida—I decided I'd better get us some friends. The case wasn't as urgent for me as it was for my mother, who at forty-seven was entering a whole new risk category based on her age.

Historically, my mother has not had great judgment when it comes to friends. She prefers Bernie to his far more orderly parents, for example. The friends who stop by after work seem to feel it is perfectly acceptable to keep their shoes on in the house, spread mustard with a communal knife, and use the bathroom without washing their hands. I always find animal hair in whatever dish Penelope brings over, and Paul has a gold tooth because the real one was knocked out in a barroom brawl!

So why was I surprised when my mother decided we should be friends with Sarah Kervick? Philosophically, I am not opposed to befriending a girl; I just did not agree on this particular girl. If my mother had asked me, I might have suggested someone like, oh, say, Glynnis Powell.

I have observed that Miss Powell wears very sensible shoes, is always neat and orderly, and does her best not to escalate tensions. She is quiet and thoughtful, not rude, law-breaking, and violent. And she understands the importance of good hygiene.

My mother, however, seemed convinced that Sarah Kervick was the one to improve our overall health profiles, going so far as to suggest that we all see a movie together sometime. A movie?? I suppose she expects us to dip our hands into the same bucket of popcorn while we're at it.

Since there were no calculations to cover this sort of dilemma, I thought it wise to consult the most brilliant statistician this nation has to offer on probable risk.

Gloria: Gloria here.
Me: Gloria, it's me. Franklin.
Gloria: What is it now, Franklin?
Me: I met a girl.
Gloria: A girl. That's a good thing.
Me: I'm not so sure, Gloria.

Gloria: Let me guess. She doesn't like you.

Me: Oh no. That's the good part. I don't like her, either. She practices very risky behaviors, Gloria.

Gloria: What *kinds* of risky behaviors?

Me: She's violent, for one thing. She punched Marvin Howerton on the school bus!

Gloria: Did he deserve it?

Me: Well . . . yes, but I hardly think that's the point. To continue, she doesn't bathe regularly. I've also noticed that she doesn't look both ways when she crosses the street. She eats breakfast and lunch at school every day. I'm sure you are aware, Gloria, of the declining quality of school lunch meat. There's quite an uproar about it in Washington.

Gloria: You sure know a lot about this girl you don't like, Franklin.

Me: But, Gloria, I'm seeing patterns here.

Gloria: Babies see patterns, Franklin.

Me: Not like me. You know that. Through careful observation, I can predict the future course of events. Remember Mr. Pitts?

Gloria: He smoked filterless cigarettes for twenty-seven years, Franklin. You hardly need to be . . . Listen, I've got a meeting in five minutes on the rising tide of personal watercraft accidents. Why don't you find something you and this young lady have in common? You like to read, for example. Maybe she likes to read, too, and you could—

Me: I'm afraid that would be impossible. I don't think she can read. At least not very well.

Gloria: How old is this girl?

Me: Eleven.

Gloria: That is a risky behavior, Franklin. Children who don't learn to read are at a disproportionately high risk of dropping out of school, ingesting illegal substances, teen pregnancy, and entering the penal system.

Me: I knew you'd understand, Gloria. If you could just pass this information on to my mother so she would see what a poor influence—

Gloria: You know what you have to do, Franklin. You have to teach this girl to read!

Me: But, Gloria!

Gloria: Meaningful volunteer work, being involved in activities that benefit others . . . these are all indicators of a long life, Franklin. I'd be happy to communicate that to your mother. Just have her call me at 1-800-555-SAFE. Good-bye, Franklin.

After I hung up the phone, I retraced the steps of our conversation to figure out just where I'd gone wrong. My intention had been to recruit Gloria to my side, to get her to assist me in helping my mother choose more appropriate friends for us. But somewhere around unfortunate, addicted Mr. Pitts, I'd lost her, gotten off track, wound up in jail instead of on Park Avenue. Now what was I supposed to do?

On the bright side, maybe I was wrong about Sarah Kervick. Maybe she could read like a college professor. But even my lively imagination couldn't work up enthusiasm for that theory. It would be, according to Franklin Delano Roosevelt, "unjustified optimism." And to date, no one has ever accused me of that.

Here is the pattern I'd observed. In school, Sarah Kervick

did not read aloud. At first, she used excuses like "I didn't bring my reading glasses" or "I'm missin' that page." Ms. Linski would sigh and say, "Use Franklin's book, then," which I would graciously offer to hand over. But Sarah would just fire right back, "It's a funny thing, Ms. Linski. He's missin' that page, too."

Then Ms. Linski would start twisting the buttons on her shirt collar and reply, "Why don't we discuss this at lunchtime, Sarah?"

"That would be fine, Ms. Linski," Sarah would say. And then she'd sit back in her seat all relaxed and relieved . . . to be in trouble!

After a while, Ms. Linski stopped calling on Sarah Kervick. She'd just skip over her. It seemed pretty obvious to me that Sarah Kervick could not read. But when Coach Jablonski showed up at the door to collect Marvin Howerton and Bryce Jordan, the remedial readers—yes, in addition to being our P.E. teacher he taught remedial reading—Sarah Kervick did not go. I wanted her to go. I got a secret feeling of pleasure thinking of the three of them, all bullies, shoehorned into the old janitor's closet that was Coach Jablonski's office.

But that is only the first pattern I saw. Sure, Sarah Kervick was a bully, but she was not disrespectful like Marvin Howerton and she didn't torment the other kids, either. Unless she wanted something. As far as I could tell, she only ever wanted things from me. But she always got in trouble. Every day. And it was always before lunch recess.

Now, why would Sarah Kervick want to stay in for recess? For someone in delicate health like me, the reasons were obvious. I was only seven when I discovered that the wood chips under the playground equipment were a full one inch short of the depth recommended by the National Playground Safety Association. In addition, the slide had no safety bars at the top. This meant that getting pushed off by children anxious to hurtle themselves down the steel chute was a very real possibility.

But, most important, the difference in the lengths of my legs made it difficult to elude the Pelican View basketball players, who seemed to make a new team sport out of reducing whatever book I was reading to shreds.

But Sarah Kervick could have none of these excuses. As far as I could tell, she wasn't afraid of anything. The word *danger* was not in her vocabulary. Still, if it was close to lunchtime and she hadn't been ordered to stay in by failing to hand in her homework or refusing to do her work in class, she would get a look on her face that was positively desperate.

What could possibly be luring her? Who did she want to see that she couldn't see during regular hours? What did she want to do that couldn't be done under the supervision of our teacher?

It was on one of those days that a curious thing happened to me. Yes, I, Franklin Delano Donuthead, felt an irresistible urge to help Sarah Kervick get recess detention and to solve, once and for all, the mystery behind her desire to stay indoors at any cost.

Ten minutes before the lunch bell rang, Sarah was shifting uneasily in her seat. That's when I leaned over to her and said, "Why don't you raise your hand and ask Ms. Linski to explain what the word *eunuch* means?"

"What?" she hissed back.

"*Eunuch*. Ask her what it means."

Kids were putting their work away in their desks, and Glynnis Powell came around collecting the milk money. I smiled up at her and shined my quarters with an anti-bacterial tissue before depositing them in her palm. Which I think she appreciated.

Then Sarah's hand shot up.

"Yes, Sarah?" Ms. Linski said, brightening. Sarah Kervick never raised her hand.

"I was just wondering, uh, what's a eunuch?"

"What's a eunuch?" she repeated, looking at Sarah with a bewildered expression on her face.

Then something really amazing happened. My hand shot up. Almost against my will, I said, "Ms. Linski, can you also explain what a hermaphrodite is?"

Ms. Linski set down her grade book and the apple-covered coffee mug she always took with her to the teachers' lounge.

"Uh, while you're at it," I finished weakly.

"Very funny, you two. I'll be happy to let you stay in for recess and look those words up in the dictionary."

"Hey, that wasn't supposed to happen," Sarah said, glaring at me and pressing her lips together to demonstrate her unhappiness.

"I thought you wanted to stay in for recess."

"Yeah, but not with you."

Were my feelings hurt? No! I was in a haze, imagining the possible consequences of my actions. As I passed into the hallway, I asked Ms. Linski if this would appear on my permanent record.

"You should have thought of that earlier, Franklin. Perhaps, in the future, you will reflect *before* you act."

Excuse me, but reflecting before I act is my specialty! I could teach master classes on the subject. What in heaven's name had gotten into me?

After lunch, Ms. Linski had the class line up for recess.

She put her hand on my shoulder and said, "Not you, Franklin. Mrs. Boardman is waiting for you in the library." She didn't even bother to include Sarah, for whom sitting in the library under the watchful eye of Mrs. Boardman was business as usual.

Mrs. Boardman did not have any children enrolled in Pelican View Elementary School. It was rumored that even her grandchildren had college diplomas by now. She had the kind of skim milk, old lady skin and powder white hair that suggested she never exposed herself to the sun, a practice I thoroughly endorse. The occurrence of melanoma, the most deadly form of skin cancer, has almost doubled since 1973.

In the entire time I have been at Pelican View Elementary, I have observed Mrs. Boardman doing only one of three things: writing notes to parents of children who have not returned their library books on time, mending torn pages with special non-yellowing Scotch tape, and reshelving the books. She never speaks, to my knowledge. Just writes note after note in her spidery handwriting: *If Billy does not return his library book forthwith, he will lose his lending privileges for the rest of the year.*

That is why I was mildly shocked when I entered the library and saw her look up in what seemed an eager way. But then she looked back down again, disappointed. It wasn't until Sarah

Kervick—who'd been walking her customary six steps away from me—appeared that she resumed her happy expression and, ignoring me completely, said in a soft, papery-thin voice, "Sarah, dear. There you are. What's been keeping you?"

Well, this was information, I told myself. Sarah Kervick had a friend. I sat down at a long, chocolate-colored table and waited to see what would happen next. But Sarah did not want to share any information with me. She walked slowly over to my table and said, "Look, Donuthead, this doesn't go anywhere. You got that? Nowhere but here. If it does . . ." She paused, considering how to drive her point home.

"Let's see," I said. "If I tell anyone that you are friends with little old lady Boardman, you'll yank my ears so hard I'll be able to tie them in a knot beneath my chin."

"Yeah. Somethin' like that."

As I glanced down at the table, I noticed that the bandages had been removed from her fingers and that her warts were nearly gone. Reflexively, she curled her fingers into fists and turned around, tossing her shiny blond hair over her shoulder.

"Hi, Grace," Sarah said when she reached Mrs. Boardman's desk.

Grace!

"Hello, Sarah." I watched in shock as Mrs. Boardman laid down her pen and put her bony hand over Sarah's. My first impulse was to warn the old woman of the dangers of infection that might still lie beneath Sarah Kervick's skin. Elderly people have compromised immune systems, you know. I did not want to be responsible for Mrs. Boardman's premature demise.

But the way she grabbed on to Sarah Kervick, I don't think she would have paid any attention to my warnings. She held her hand and spoke to her in a low voice.

"I was able to get over to that library in Wing Rock. Mr. Benkert, my neighbor, had to visit his mother up that way. Poor dear broke another hip. But just you see what I got you." And she smiled a smile broad enough to crack her face, then rose slowly, pulled a key from her pocket, and shuffled over to the closet that held the coat and hat and briefcase of the regular librarian, Mrs. Fox. Unlocking the door, Mrs. Boardman took a cloth sack from behind the lost and found box.

"Here it is."

I was expecting something exotic, like maybe a book on medieval torture or ancient Egyptian burial rites. Almost against my will, I rose in my seat to get a better look. As if sensing my movement, Sarah Kervick's head shot around with the glare of Medusa and froze me to the spot.

She turned back to Mrs. Boardman and said, "How long can we keep it, do you think?"

"It depends on when they move Mrs. Benkert. I'd say we have it until next Friday, at least."

Sarah Kervick held the book tightly to her chest and moved over to the picture book area. Then she flopped down on her stomach, and all I could see were the bottoms of her worn tennis shoes.

I became absolutely consumed with discovering the book that made Sarah Kervick relax her hunched-up shoulders and smile so sweetly.

It was a strange sensation, much like the one that had

55

caused me to raise my hand and voluntarily get recess detention. You see, normally I don't feel curiosity about things that are not connected to my personal safety. In fact, I like to arrange situations so that I have as much control as possible.

But the more I tried to arrange things around Sarah Kervick, the less control there was to be had. Something told me I was entering a whole new area of danger, and this was not physical! Libraries are, statistically, very safe places to be, unless you misuse the step stools that are intended for staff use only.

I rose from my seat and approached Mrs. Boardman. The reference section formed a wall that blocked my view of the picture book area. If I could just get to it, I could peek over and . . .

"Yes, Franklin?" Mrs. Boardman said, looking up at me from her work.

"I was wondering, Mrs. Boardman," I said loudly. "Do you have any statistics on the rising tide of personal watercraft accidents?"

She blinked at me a few times. "Well, we have *The Guinness Book of World Records*."

"I see . . . and that would be . . ."

She pointed to nonfiction. Opposite direction.

"I see," I said, casting a meaningful glance over her shoulder.

She raised one eyebrow, just for a second, and then said, a little more loudly, "But if you are looking for tragic domestic accidents, which I understand is a personal interest of yours, I might recommend *The Three Little Pigs* in the folktale section at the far corner of the picture book area."

"That was tragic indeed," I said, smiling up at Mrs. Boardman. "I'll look that up right away." And I stepped right over Sarah Kervick's legs on the way to the folktales.

In between doing some research for my list of characters who might die from preventable accidents—Why did Little Red Riding Hood have to talk to strangers? Why did Goldilocks have to trespass?—I managed to steal several glances at Sarah Kervick.

As I had suspected, it was an oversize picture book, full of—of all things—figure skaters looping and twirling and bending over in ways that would exert dangerous pressure on the lumbar region of the spine.

Normally, she might have been bothered that I was so close to her without being invited. But this book had clearly taken Sarah Kervick far away into some frosty daydream of her own. Why did she want to go so badly that she would let down her guard like this?

We passed the whole of recess that way, the three of us quietly rustling pages until the bell rang. It was very peaceful.

Reluctantly, Sarah handed the book back to Mrs. Boardman, who returned it to her bag.

"Growing up in Norway," she told Sarah, "the only way to get to school in winter was by skating down the frozen river. Mama gave us each a potato from the fire to put in our pocket. That kept our little fingers from getting frostbite."

"You were poor, weren't you?" Sarah Kervick asked.

"Yes, dear. We were very poor."

•••

The halls had pretty much emptied out by the time we left the library. I walked quickly back to class, anxious to be reinstated in the good graces of Ms. Linski. After all, I am known for returning from recess in a timely manner, and I considered it a point of honor to uphold this standard of excellence.

But something told me to look back for Sarah Kervick. She was standing motionless in front of the plate glass window by the office. The same window that gave Mr. Putman a full view of the playground.

"It's your pal Bernie," she said, squinting into the distance. A broad grin broke across her face. "And my pal Marvin Howerton." With a jerk of her thumb, she called out, "C'mon."

Every gene in my risk-averse body told me to proceed calmly toward the fifth-grade classroom, where after-lunch silent reading would already have begun. Then I began the now-familiar "get back" calculation, which was the proportion of Sarah Kervick's anger roughly divided by the number of bones in my body to the square root of my ability to withstand pain.

I followed her out the door.

She had located them in a small corner of the playground supposedly reserved for rousing games of four square. I knew the walls that flanked the playing area intimately. When a smallish person is pushed up against one, it is impossible for Mr. Putman to see from his vantage point in the office.

The recess aides had already filed in with the other kids, and the yard was strangely still. The immediate sensation of my impending doom kept me from being too concerned about being caught on the playground after recess.

"Give me back my cards," Bernie was saying. "I need those cards."

It's a well-known fact that Bernie Lepner makes his own playing cards. The Lepner deck consists of seventy-two cards with pictures from *National Geographic* Mod Podged onto the fronts of real playing cards. I myself have inhaled the fumes while he created them at our kitchen table. Using these cards, players make up stories, based on the hands they are dealt. The game has certain possibilities, particularly when one is dealt pictures of natural catastrophes. The cards travel with Bernie everywhere, carefully secured by a rubber band and stuffed into his back pants pocket.

"What's up, Bernie?" Sarah asked, shouldering her way into the circle created by Bernie, Marvin Howerton, and Bryce Jordan, his best friend and partner in crime. I hung back at a respectful distance.

Despite the cold weather, Bernie's face was damp with sweat, his long bangs plastered over his eyes.

"They took my cards, Sarah."

"We're gonna make a house of cards," Marvin said. "After school."

"Then there's gonna be a house fire," Bryce added, waving the deck in the air before letting it drop to the ground. His other hand was on Bernie's shoulder, pressing him into the brick.

"That's very interesting," Sarah Kervick said, rubbing her chin. "But I think there's gonna be a problem with that plan."

I continued to hang back, desperate to concoct a way to alert the proper authorities.

"Yeah? What's that?" Bryce wanted to know.

Sarah Kervick was taking her time.

" 'Cause Bernie here is Donuthead's friend, and Donuthead doesn't want you messin' with Bernie. Isn't that right?" she said, looking back at me, then tossing her head at them. It was a silent invitation.

One that I declined.

"Well," I stammered. "In point of fact, Bernie and I are, officially, neighbors. I'm not sure we qualify . . . yet . . . as close personal friends." My head wagged back and forth between Bryce and Sarah and Marvin, trying to decide who was the most dangerous. They ended in a draw, which was why I kept stammering even after all useful syllables had drained from the part of my brain that controls speech.

It was hopeless to keep all three of them from inflicting bodily harm on me. I knew this, and I now admit, almost shamefully, that I wasn't thinking too much about Bernie or his precious cards.

I had the instincts of the gazelle, all right.

That is, until Bernie said, "It's okay, Franklin, Sarah. You guys go on inside. I can handle this."

The "go on inside" was uttered in a serious, almost parental tone, as if Bernie wanted us to understand the dangerous nature of his work here. From his position, pinned beneath Bryce's beefy paw, it seemed like a clear-cut case of unjustified optimism to me.

It also made me feel like a lousy worm.

"Yeah, we can handle this," Bryce said, giving Sarah a push with his free hand. Her shoulder swung back at the pressure, but she held her ground.

"Let me rephrase that," I said, raising my eyebrows in Sarah's direction. "Bernie *is* my friend, and despite the obvious outcome of this little speech, I'm afraid I'll have to ask you to return his cards, or . . ."

"Or what?" Marvin Howerton now grabbed my shoulder and began applying pressure. I felt faint. I think I swooned.

"Trouble is, we can't fight you fair," Sarah said. "Me and Bernie and Donuthead here got you outnumbered."

"Guess we'll have to take our chances," Marvin replied, squeezing ever harder. In another life, he might have been a boa constrictor.

"Okay then, since you're such a big guy, I'll let you go with Bernie and Donuthead. But Bryce's gotta put those cards on the ledge over there so they're safe. After we fight, winner take all."

Sarah had both hands on her hips. It was clear she meant business.

Events were moving far too quickly for my liking. After all, we hadn't exhausted negotiations yet, had we?

"That's reasonable," Marvin said, and nodded to Bryce, who picked up the pack and slid it onto the window ledge. "Why not? It's worth it to see the kid fight."

Reasonable? We're talking about soft tissues here!

"I haven't seen him take a swing in six years," Bryce added, his voice tinged with nostalgia.

I could feel my pupils dilating.

Sarah smiled sweetly. "It's a funny thing how you don't

fight fair," she said to Marvin, "pickin' on little kids and cripples and all. I guess that means I don't have to fight fair, either."

And before any of us could react, she'd turned sideways and shoved her elbow right into the doughy part of Marvin's stomach. He let go of me with an *oooff* and dropped to his knees, clutching his stomach.

"You act kinda slow to understand that," she said, looking down at him.

After a moment of stunned silence, Bryce sprang into action, releasing Bernie and reattaching himself to Sarah's hair.

"Let her go!" Bernie screamed dramatically and threw himself onto Bryce's back, pulling on his scalp like a pro wrestler in training. I was doing the tail end of the Virginia reel from the massive push I'd gotten when Marvin went down. I had just reestablished my equilibrium when I heard Sarah cry out.

Whether it was pain or a battle cry, I never did figure out. Marvin had struggled to his feet and made a grab for Sarah. He missed.

At the same time that Bryce smacked her hard on the side of the head, Sarah ground her flimsy little tennis shoe into Marvin's instep. Then Bernie covered Bryce's eyes with his hands, while Sarah recovered enough to deliver another quick elbow, this time to Bryce's stomach. In order to avoid being flattened, Bernie abandoned ship as Bryce went down.

While Marvin clutched his foot, nursing the pain of his fallen arch, I got the chance to witness the famous ground-floor punch. It started somewhere by Sarah Kervick's shin and found its target on Marvin's chin. He sprawled out on the cement, a part of his body in each square of the four square diagram.

Bernie rushed over to Sarah, who had staggered to the wall and was leaning up against it.

And so it was over in mere seconds. Marvin was on the ground, tears in his eyes. Bryce was searching for the hole in his stomach. The episode was too short for me to see active duty, though I did reflexively raise my hands to my face a couple of times.

I am proud to say I held my ground.

"Where I come from, they teach the dirty tricks," Sarah said, out of breath, to the reclining giants. "I can show you some more if you want. They're kinda like magic tricks. Only they hurt."

She reached over and picked up Bernie's cards, dusting them off and smoothing out the bent corners.

"Now, Bernie, you go to class and me and Donuthead'll go to class and we'll tell Ms. Linski you boys are with the nurse or somethin'. We'll tell her you don't feel so good."

Sarah walked away, resisting the urge to touch her cheek, which was already sprouting a goose egg.

"Thanks, Sarah," Bernie said, giving her the look he usually reserved for my mother.

"You got promise, Bernie. I mean that," she said.

I knew I should apologize. I was nothing but a liability in playground skirmishes. But I am a pacifist, after all. Your values aren't tested until the going gets rough, right?

"Why?" I asked Sarah once we were back in the building. "Why did you help Bernie like that?"

"Good question, comin' from you," she said. Then she shrugged. "The kid's my friend."

"But you just met him the other day."

"'Cause he's your mom's friend, then, that's how come. And she's my friend."

We were passing through the lower elementary. Ms. Karwowski, the second-grade teacher, had rows and rows of painted sunflowers displayed outside her room. I looked at Sarah Kervick against the backdrop of all those pretty yellow flowers. There was no other way to explain it. What she did for Bernie was kind.

"Should we get some ice for that?" I asked, pointing to her swollen cheek.

"Nah. I had worse." She was walking fast ahead of me, the torn pocket of her jeans flipping back and forth with her stride.

She was not a lioness. And she was definitely not a gazelle. As we reached Ms. Linski's classroom, I realized I was going to need a whole new theory now that Sarah Kervick had reached the jungles of Pelican View Elementary.

CHAPTER SIX

Spring Training

In emergency situations, total strangers can become best friends. Burning buildings, sinking ships. There's a powerful urge to believe that those who may be sharing your final moments are your nearest and dearest. I admit to having a few soft feelings for Sarah Kervick after she rescued Bernie and his cards from the troglodyte twins. I thought she was noble to go out of her way to see him to safety. With her as my protector, I could envision a future in which my resting pulse rate was the same at school as on a lazy Sunday afternoon. And so the next day, when she began to follow me home, I felt a mixture of affection and sympathy for the way she'd so quickly attached herself to my mother and me.

But apparently Sarah Kervick had not undergone the same transformation. Maybe she did not consider what had happened on the playground a near-death experience. Maybe she did not have normal human feelings. After all, we have already established that she did not feel pain or fear.

She walked the traditional six steps away from me in silence all the way home. When I edged a little closer in order to strike up a conversation, she widened the gap. Upon reaching the house, she did not turn around and wait for me to invite her in; she rang the bell.

"My mother's not home," I told her. "She works until four on Thursday."

"Oh," she said, sitting down on the frozen step. "Okay. I'll wait."

I thought of what my mother might do to me if she found a half-frozen Sarah Kervick on her doorstep.

"You can wait inside, you know," I said. "I won't hurt you."

Sarah nearly leapt off the step. "It's a deal," she said. "I won't hurt you, either."

She perched herself on a barstool in the kitchen while I hung up my jacket. Then I began to wash my hands.

"Is it your birthday?" she asked as I dried each finger individually with my extra-absorbent, waffle-weave towel.

"No," I said. I was about to explain the importance of good hygiene and extended contact with anti-bacterial soap when I realized I was the host here. Shouldn't I offer her something? In my short and uneventful life, I had never willingly invited someone over to my house before. It's true that Bernie came over to watch the Disney Channel, since the Lepners were philosophically opposed to anything beyond basic cable. Did that count?

"Let's see," I said now, going over in my mind all the snacks my mother had purchased against my advice. "How about some Oreos?"

"Okay." Sarah didn't seem as hungry as the first couple of times she came over. Carefully, she pulled two from the package and placed them on a plate I'd given her. She ate slowly with her head down.

I think we were both relieved to see my mother's van pull

into the driveway. Sarah jumped off the barstool and flicked at her dress to make sure she was crumb-free. We stood there, both of us fixated on the door, when my mother walked in.

She didn't seem at all surprised to see us in the kitchen together.

"Hey, Sarah," was what my mother said as she opened the fridge and pulled out a pitcher of iced tea.

"I was just wonderin'," Sarah began, giving me the now-familiar sideways glance that communicated there was no earthly reason—in her mind—why I had been put on the planet. "The thing is, I—"

There was an urgent knock on the storm door. We turned to see Bernie's palms flat up against the glass.

"That you, Franklin?" he shouted, getting his spit all over the door.

My mother put up a finger in Sarah's direction.

"Come on in, Bern," she called.

He didn't come in, exactly. Bernie stood in the doorway, half in, half out, letting the cold air exchange places with the temperate air in our climate-controlled hallway.

"Franklin," he said, all breathless. "You better come quick." Then his eyes fell on Sarah and he seemed to lose all sense of urgency.

"Sarah," he said, gazing at her with a dreamy smile.

My mother put down the pitcher of iced tea, and we all waited for Bernie to say something more.

He straightened up and smoothed down his bangs. "I just want to say you look exactly like Alice in Wonderland with your hair all pretty like that."

"Thanks," Sarah said, looking at the ground. While I wasn't close enough to guarantee this, I think she blushed.

"Bernie, honey," my mother said to snap him out of his trance. "What were you going to say to Franklin?"

"Oh! Mr. Nillson is painting his garage on a stepladder, Franklin, right near the electrical wires."

"Wood or metal?"

"Huh?"

"The stepladder."

"It's metal." He grabbed my newly sanitized wrist with his grubby hand. "You've got to talk some sense into him!" Bernie pulled me to the door but paused before he plunged into the cold outside air.

"I can get my pack of cards and we can act out a scene from the book, if you want, Sarah. Maybe the part where Alice meets the Cheshire Cat, or where Alice has tea with the Mad Hatter. Afterwards . . . on the front steps."

Later, I reflected that while I probably saved Mr. Nillson from an untimely heart attack—Hello! Those wires were not grounded—it was a small consolation for the conversation I missed at my house.

In *my* kitchen, calmly sipping iced tea and nibbling Oreo cookies, my mother listened to Sarah's problems. I bet it took about a second for her to decide to put *my life* on the line so that Sarah Kervick could have "a chance at bein' regular."

Yes, as I was trying to save yet another hapless neighbor from a tragic domestic accident, Sarah was telling my mother that she needed a job so she could buy clothes that made her look more like the other girls—though why that would be her aim, I can't imagine.

Did my mother have any ideas, she wondered.

Oh, yes, indeed she did.

Finally, my mother had found someone desperate enough to recruit into her evil plan of putting me on the Pelican View Baseball Team.

"I bet she doesn't know a thing about baseball," I said when she told me about how she'd hired Sarah to help us with practices.

"Doesn't matter," my mother shot back. "I can't pitch and catch at the same time."

"What about Bernie? Let him be catcher."

"Very funny. We already tried that, remember? He set up his plastic animals at home plate and I almost gave him a concussion."

Three fleeting days later, I stood on home plate, looking over the vast expanse of desert that was the Paul I. Phillips Recreation League infield. Official practice had not yet begun for the season, so the chalk lines were barely visible and the area around home plate was rutted from dirt bike tires. Sarah sat in the bleachers, her arms folded out of habit or cold, but definitely not stubbornness. Not this time, anyway. Wasn't she getting what she wanted?

Overnight, my mother had transformed into a baseball coach. She leapt from her van, went around to the back, and pulled out a huge duffel bag with what looked like a dead body flopping around inside. Dumping the contents on the field, she motioned Sarah over.

"Here's your first installment," she said, producing a padded green nylon jacket with about seventeen pockets and as many zippers. I was all set to issue a standard safety warning about the dangers of loose ties and zippers when boarding the school bus when the look on Sarah's face kept my thoughts from connecting to my mouth. It was the sort of look I imagine Cinderella having when her fairy godmother conjures up the amazing gown for the ball.

Pulling off her ratty, unraveling sweater, Sarah dropped it in the dirt by the batter's box. Gingerly, she slid one arm into the jacket sleeve. Halfway through the procedure, she bit her lip and looked down at the ground.

"Thanks," she mumbled, and I could tell she was close to tears, so I limped away to distribute the bases. My mother busied herself unpacking the rest of the bag.

"This is for you, Franklin," she said, holding up the traditional batter's helmet with the protective disk that dipped down over the exposed ear.

Standard issue safety equipment could hardly be considered a generous gift under the circumstances, but I tried to look grateful.

My mother and I had had a long talk the evening before.

"Look, Franklin," she said. "I just want to do something normal for once. Just a normal mother and son kind of thing. No crash dummies, no fatality statistics, just . . . I don't know . . . typical."

In my mind, I searched crazily for a sport or activity that was completely safe, that we could both enjoy without fear. And to my horror, I discovered there wasn't one. Everything that flashed through my mind—street fairs, bowling, nature center hikes—sent up red flags of danger.

There must be something, I reasoned. Finally, it came.

"As long as it is combined with a sensible exercise program and done in the comfort of your home, I would say that reading is a perfectly safe hobby for us to share."

My mother looked disgusted. "You're wrong," she said finally. "Reading can be very dangerous. Authors can get people very worked up with their writing. Reading has caused revolutions, Franklin.

"Even FDR didn't trust reading. Don't you remember his annual address of 1944? He had the flu, so he insisted that the radio program be broadcast from his bed in the White House rather than have people read about the speech in the newspaper?"

"I'm not sure he was actually in bed . . ."

"Don't try to distract me with details, young man. The fact is, reading is one of the most dangerous things around."

"I wasn't talking about *that* kind of dangerous," I argued. "I was talking about the getting-hit-by-a-line-drive kind of dangerous. Physical dangerous."

"What difference does it make? A guy could die of a broken heart after reading a Dear John letter. A story in the newspaper could cause a riot."

She was just being stubborn, and she was old enough to know it.

"Fine. I give. Uncle. Reading is more dangerous than stock car driving."

"I'm just trying to make a point, Franklin. Anything is

dangerous if you look at it a certain way. Just getting up in the morning is dangerous."

"Exactly!" I said. "We're in total agreement."

But I knew we weren't. And my mother knew we weren't, so I had to keep returning to the subject and mulling it over.

Was it possible that I, Franklin Delano Donuthead, could be overreacting to the dangers of childhood, as my mother was suggesting? Why wasn't my mother overjoyed to have a son who took such diligent care of himself? Was there something I was missing here? Was something greater expected of me? Was the maternal pleasure of watching a son field a hard grounder down the third base line more important than taking precautions to ensure that same son survive to adulthood?

When I agreed to her plan, I have to admit that my mother looked happier with me than she had in a long time. And happiness, according to Gloria Nelots, is a major boost to longevity.

"Okay, kids," my mother said now, leaning on two bats, one wooden, one aluminum. "Here are the ground rules. We've got three weeks before baseball season officially starts. Our goal is to get Franklin enough skills so that he feels comfortable signing up. We'll practice every day after school for one hour, except Thursday, when I work late."

Sarah's hand shot up. "Me and Donuthead, I mean, Franklin, can practice on our own on Thursday. You okay with that?" she said to me in her own agree-or-I'll-rearrange-your-body-parts kind of way.

I attempted to give my mother a see-what-I-have-to-put-up-with look, but she would not make eye contact.

"Great," she said. "That's great. And, Sarah, I'm going to have to talk to your parents about this."

Before Sarah could disguise her reaction as anger, a troubled look crossed her face. Then she sat right down on the cold ground and hugged her knees.

"I can't be keeping you after school and sending you home with clothes without their permission, dear," my mother said, kneeling beside Sarah and resting one hand on her bony knee.

"Him, it's just him. My dad," Sarah said quietly. She was shaking her head and dragging her finger through the wet sand near her feet. When she finally did look at my mother, it was like Sarah was trying to decide if she was poisonous or not.

"Okay," she said finally. "Whatever."

"All right, then." My mother slapped Sarah's knee and sprang up. "Let's play ball. We'll start with batting practice." She tossed the catcher's mitt to Sarah. "I'll pitch. Franklin, which do you prefer? Aluminum or wood?"

I opened my mouth to explain that either instrument, when applied with the proper force, could prove deadly. But as I watched my mother dance out to the pitcher's mound, I didn't have the heart to say it. I set the batting helmet on my head. It tilted to one side, exposing my left earlobe.

"I may have to have this fitted correctly before we begin," I announced. My mother jogged back to home plate and slapped the top of my head. While this did help with placement, it seemed unnecessarily cruel. Now my ears were ringing.

"Sarah," she called out, "you stand here, behind Franklin. Okay, now squat down and put the mitt between your legs."

"Hey, my new jacket could get dirty," Sarah complained, stopping at a bend.

My mother sighed. "That's one of the dangers of baseball. You might get dirty."

Sarah stood up, pulled off her jacket, and hung it on the chain-link fence. Then she returned to squat in the dirt behind me, pushing her flimsy dress down between her knees.

"That's right," my mother said, "but bring the mitt higher. Gives me a target to aim for."

For a moment, she looked at us the way you do pictures in the art museum that you can't quite figure out. Then she dropped her glove and walked back over to me.

"Now, Franklin, we've been over this before, but just for review . . . ," she began.

How many times my mother had tried to get me in this position I could not tell you. I make every effort to block out painful experiences. In fact, I think I can trace the onset of my post-traumatic stress disorder to the first time she pitched me a softball.

"This is the strike zone," she said, touching my shoulders and my knees. "When the ball is thrown between these two points, a good ump will call a strike. That means you should swing at it, because if you don't, they're going to hold it against you."

"Why do they call it a strike if it means you *don't* hit the ball? In the dictionary, *strike* means 'to hit, with a hand, tool, or weapon.'"

"Quit stallin'. We're gonna play ball whether you recite the dictionary or not. I don't plan to be in this position all day," I heard Sarah's voice behind me.

"Okay now, Franklin," my mother said, trying to recover her earlier enthusiasm. "You know the drill. Feet shoulder-width apart, bend your knees . . . no, that's a slight forward bend." She twisted me like a pretzel.

"Wouldn't common sense dictate that I lean away from the strike zone, rather than into it?"

Huge sigh. "Franklin, imagine you want to hit the ball as opposed to avoiding it. Imagine that you want to get that offending ball as far away from you as possible."

"There's an easy solution to that," I said, taking a step back.

"No, dear," she said, firmly propelling me forward. She walked backward to the pitcher's mound, just to make sure I stayed.

"Don't balance the bat on your shoulder, cock your elbow in the direction of the pitcher, watch the ball . . ."

Her words crackled around me like static electricity as I entered into an advanced state of panic.

"Try to remember what FDR said, Franklin." My mother pulled the implement of destruction out of the duffel bag and stepped onto the pitcher's mound. "The only thing you have to fear is fear itself."

I thought I detected a slight tremor in the ground below me. She threw the ball directly at me and I jumped away, dropping the bat. In the distance, I heard a thud as the missile found its mark in Sarah Kervick's palm.

"Are you all right?" I shouted, craning my neck to see her. My mother started toward us, but Sarah tossed back the ball and held up her finger, as if to say, *Just give me a minute here.*

"I have an idea." She stood up and stepped around me.

Keeping her back to my mother, she said, "Look here. If you don't learn to play ball, I don't get any clothes. If I don't get any clothes, I walk around lookin' like this. If I walk around lookin' like this just because you don't learn to play ball, then we have a problem. Because then I'm gonna be very angry. And there is nothing this ball can do to you that my fist can't do better and harder and more times. . . ."

"There seems to be a pattern here," I said, impressed with Sarah Kervick's abilities at deductive reasoning. "Where you threaten me so that I do what you say. You never actually hurt me, though, do you?"

"There's a reason for that, too. As a rule, I don't hit cripples. But just remember what I did to Marvin Howerton. Twice. 'Cause that's what happens when I get angry. And I do get angry, Franklin. Even cripples make me angry."

I was strangely touched that she recognized that I am, indeed, a handicapped person. I glanced over her shoulder at my mother, who was rubbing the ball up and down her jeans, waiting patiently.

"I think you need a new strategy for communicating," I said. "If you want to be regular, like you keep saying, then you should learn to persuade people without threatening them."

Sarah Kervick sighed heavily and scuffed her dirty old tennis shoe in the sand. She did want to be regular, I could tell.

"Should I say please?" she asked through gritted teeth. "Is that what you're sayin'? Because if you will step up there and try to hit the ball if I say please, then I'll say it."

"Please would help."

"Okay, then. Please."

I stepped away from her and approached home plate. I got into the batter's stance. My mother had one of those looks that you see at the end of movies, when you know the baby's going to live. I tried to remind myself that, statistically speaking, my chances for surviving this practice were excellent, and that my chances would increase if I could focus on the movement of the ball.

I willed myself to lean forward and concentrate. Really this was very simple if I just broke it down into a physics problem. This was all about velocity. My bat would repel this sphere at high velocity.

My mother wound up. Despite my mental preparations, I froze in position as the ball sailed past, dangerously close to my nose. But I didn't step back or drop the bat, which was, I believe, a minor victory worth celebrating.

Sarah tossed the ball back to my mother. We repeated this exercise several times. Everyone seemed to understand that a person with my delicate constitution required a great deal of warming up.

In between watching the ball sail past my nose, I swung the bat for practice. It occurred to me that if I kept this up for a long period of time, the muscles in my left arm might lengthen, while the muscles in my right arm could foreshorten, thereby increasing the difference in the lengths of my arms.

"Do we need to have another talk?" Sarah Kervick asked, interrupting my thoughts.

"No," I said firmly, and settled back into my stance. As I watched the ball come toward me once again, I thought, Motion, friction, velocity, speed, acceleration. I didn't close my eyes until the moment of impact. When I opened them, the ball was dribbling toward the pitcher's mound.

Both Sarah Kervick and my mother leapt into the air and cheered.

"You hit the ball, Franklin!" my mother screamed, running toward me and picking me up.

"Well, I think that's enough for one day," I responded, trying to use all those good feelings to my advantage.

My mother finished swinging me around and dropped me, unceremoniously, onto the ground so she could consult her watch. "We still have a little time. Sarah, you want to give it a try?"

Sarah had retreated to the fence to gaze lovingly at her new jacket.

"I guess," she said, as if she didn't care at all.

My mother held out both bats, offering Sarah her choice of wood or aluminum.

"What do you use?" she asked my mother.

"I guess I like wood better," my mother said.

"All right, then." Sarah took the wood bat and strolled back to the batter's box. I started to pry the helmet off my head.

"Keep it," she said over her shoulder.

"You'll catch, Franklin?"

My mother tossed me the mitt like this was not a matter for lengthy discussion.

Talk about a roller coaster of emotion. I went from surviving a ball thrown toward me to having it thrown directly at me!

"Isn't there a mask for catchers?" I asked, "to protect the soft tissues of the face?"

"Just hold your mitt up, Franklin," my mother said.

I was about to point out that if I protected my face with the mitt, I would not be able to see the ball. But then I was distracted by a new concern. What was the probability of contracting a fungal virus from sharing a mitt with Sarah Kervick? While I was trying to work out this possibility, the ball came zooming toward me.

I screamed and fell backward, crushing my shoulder in the hard-packed sand. Sarah stepped over me to retrieve the ball.

"You okay?" she asked, without much interest. On the way back, she reached out her hand. Without thinking, I took it and let her help me up.

"If you don't scream," she said quietly, "I can probably hit it. Then you won't have to catch it."

She said this almost nicely, as if she were trying to help me.

"But keep your head down. I swing low."

So I crouched there, thinking of turtles and trying to retract my head into my shoulder blades.

What I saw then was a beautiful demonstration of motion, friction, velocity, speed, acceleration. For Sarah Kervick cracked that ball so hard it sailed over my mother's head, over second base, and into the outer outfield.

And for some reason, I thought again about Marvin Howerton's nose. And his chin. And believe it or not, I almost felt sorry for the guy.

Skating on Thin Ice

I was not forced to dodge any more pitches that day. Head, shoulders, knees, or sweet spot, wherever my mother pitched the ball, Sarah met it with her bat and sent it flying. Tired of jogging all over creation, my mother finally sent me to the outfield, where a kid has at least a decent chance of avoiding the ball.

Sarah would simply smack the ball, then watch as my mother and I scrambled to keep up with it, leaning on her bat with one leg crossed over the other, a patient smile on her face. After a dozen or so hits, my mother jogged to the plate. Practice was over.

"Holy crow," she said, bending down and putting her hand by Sarah's footprint. "Where'd you learn to hit like that?"

"I used to play some."

My mother studied her hand, then went over to her duffel bag, pulled out her Cable Country receipt pad, and wrote a note along the bottom.

"Tomorrow, we'll see if you can run."

I think we both knew the "you" she was referring to. I felt grateful to Sarah Kervick for taking the pressure off me.

We packed up the equipment and got into Mother's van. Sarah sat in front so she could give directions. I didn't pay much attention to where we were headed. I was busy reliving the afternoon and my own successes. Okay, they were minor compared with Sarah Kervick's hit parade, but I had met one of my mother's wicked fastballs, hadn't I? I felt the need to communicate the importance of this moment to someone who could appreciate it. I began to calculate just how I could sneak in a toll-free call before dinner to Gloria when the van hit a pothole and we began bouncing down a rutted dirt road.

Every so often there'd be an opening in the trees and I would get a glimpse of metal or aluminum siding. We weren't in a trailer park exactly, more like a clump of woods where trailers had come to rest in no particular order.

"It's in here," Sarah said, waving her hand. My mother turned into a clearing that held a small trailer supported on cement blocks.

"You sure you want to do this?" Sarah asked.

"Of course I'm sure—"

Suddenly, from both sides of the car, huge dogs came lunging at us, barking like the van was full of fresh meat and we were downwind. My mother slammed on the brakes just as they hit the van, rocking it with their enormous paws.

"I'll handle it," Sarah said, unlocking the door. To my horror, she stepped out of the van, leaving the door open! The dogs left off mauling the van and lunged at her. For a moment, we lost her in a flurry of paws and dog hair.

"Mom," I screamed. "Do something!"

"Pretzel! Zero!" I could still hear Sarah's voice over the sounds of gnashing teeth and frenzied barking. After several long seconds, she managed to get hold of the dogs by wrapping her bony arms around their necks and grabbing the metal-studded collars.

"Hey, it's me. C'mon, c'mon."

They must have listened. I don't know how you can wrestle two dogs twice your size into a pen if they don't have any respect for you.

It was only when the immediate danger of being pulled out of the van and devoured by starving dogs was gone that I realized what a stew pot of germs, insects, and domestic accidents was the place that Sarah Kervick must call home. The tiny, rusted trailer seemed to rise up out of a whole bunch of rusty things, like automobile parts and skeletons of lawn mowers.

I hoped, for her sake, that Sarah Kervick had had her tetanus shot.

The screen door flapped open and smacked against the side of the trailer so that the whole place shook. A small, balding man stood at the door. He was wearing an open flannel shirt and a pair of dirty jeans and rubbing his eyes.

"What the . . . Sarah! What are you doin' to those dogs? I told you—" He stopped when he saw my mother approach. By this time she'd gotten out of the van and—I cringed—was holding out her hand to shake his.

"Who are you? Nothin' wrong with my cable, is there? Now, don't be disconnectin' me. I paid up at the Family Fare this morning after work . . ."

I cracked the window to hear better.

Sarah flew around the side of the van. "Dad, this is the lady I was tellin' you about. The one that gave me the hair stuff."

Sarah Kervick's father—would that be Mr. Kervick?—swept his daughter aside, keeping his eyes on my mother. He was awake now, and I could tell he was suspicious of her. My mother just stood there with her hand extended. Against all good reason, I wanted him to reach out and shake hands with her. She looked foolish offering for so long.

But little things like etiquette didn't seem to matter to Sarah's father.

"What'd you bring her here for?" he asked Sarah.

"She didn't bring me here. I asked to come," my mother said calmly.

"We don't need no help, lady."

"I'm not offering any." My mother is a patient woman. She put her hand down and leaned up against the side of the van, waiting.

"She's givin' me a job, Dad . . ."

"With your permission."

"Shut up," he said, speaking to his daughter as if we weren't there. "I know about these people. They come round askin' questions. That's first. Then they pretend they want to help ya, but . . ." He looked at my mother again.

"Look, lady, we don't got lice. She goes to school. Why don't you get the hell off my property?"

"Dad, it's not like that . . ." Sarah tried again.

"Whadda you know about it?" he asked. And when he raised his hand to his head, Sarah ducked. Mr. Kervick scratched behind his ear. I sank back in my seat.

He stared hard, first at his daughter, then at the van with the Cable Country logo on the side and my mother's uniform with her name embroidered over the pocket.

"Who's he?" he asked, zeroing in on the backseat.

"That's Donuthead," Sarah said. "I told you about him."

The wind was playing with the screen door and it kept bumping into him. He took his fist and banged it aside. Sarah flinched again.

"The cripple?"

I tried to squeeze up my courage to tell him I preferred the word *handicapped,* but none came.

"Actually, he's just scared," my mother said.

"Scared? Scared a what?"

"Everything."

He laughed at that. At least part of him did. The other part started to cough, a low, rumbling smoker's cough. Fishing in the pocket of his shirt, he sank down onto the cement block steps, gently pressing on the block at his feet to stay balanced.

My mother waited for him to stop coughing. We all waited as the unlit cigarette waved in the air and he pounded on his chest. When he finally got the space to breathe again, he lit up, straightening, wiping the tears from his eyes.

Exhaling smoke, he said, "They make some pair, don't they?"

"How's that?" my mother asked.

"He's afraid of every little thing and my Sarah, she's not afraid of nothin'."

"He's not afraid of everything. That's not true," Sarah said. She was moving all over the yard now, first tossing the dogs a stick the size of a two-by-four and letting them worry it between them, then perching on the step next to her father.

I thought her comment deserved follow-up, but apparently no one else did. Mr. Kervick gave my mother another long, hard look. "If you *are* one of them social service people dressed up like the cable guy, then I gotta hand it to you," he said.

"Everybody's afraid of something," my mother said quietly.

"That so?" he said, inhaling so hard I was afraid the cigarette would shoot to the back of his mouth.

"Your daughter's afraid you're going to say no. She's afraid of that right now."

I watched the look on Sarah's face as my mother said that. I watched her clench and unclench her fists. But all that energy had nowhere to go. You can't stick your fist into something like a feeling. There's just nothing there to hit.

"I'm talkin' about real fear, miss," her father said, picking threads of tobacco off his tongue and rubbing them on his pants. "The kind that grabs your throat in the middle of the night." He started to get up, casting his eyes left and right as if he were planning to show us what he meant.

"And you're afraid that she'll change so much you'll lose her."

It was not the kind of comment to de-escalate tensions.

"You're dead wrong if you think that," he said calmly, pushing off the step and straightening up as he walked over to face my mother. "You can't lose somethin' you don't have."

A breeze lifted the tails of his shirt, and Sarah's father looked old then, with his gray-haired chest displayed for all the world to see.

"Only person Sarah belongs to is Sarah. Ain't that right, kid?" He grabbed her roughly by the shoulder and pulled her toward him. "She's crazy, this kid. Won't back down for nothin'."

Sarah looked down at the ground, smiled, and kicked a clod of dirt.

"Give you an example. There's a pond back of this trailer park," he said, letting go of Sarah's shoulder and jabbing his lit cigarette in the direction of the woods. "Just last fall, she fell through the ice. Coulda drown, but she's got this idea she's gonna be—"

"Dad! Look, can I work for the clothes or can't I? Franklin and his mom don't got all day." Sarah waved her hand in front of him, trying to bring him back to the beginning of the conversation.

Her interruption seemed to confuse him. He blinked at her and threw his cigarette aside, continuing his story somewhere further along than when he'd left it.

"Coupla weeks later, that pond froze again and she was right back at it."

"The clothes, Dad. Can I or can't I?" She was tugging on his sleeve now. "I'm gonna earn 'em fair and square."

My mother pushed herself away from the side of the van and moved to the little space beside Mr. Kervick and his daughter. I could hear her keys jangle as she pulled them out of her pocket.

"When there's no ice, she's at it on that flat spot where I used to park my RV . . ." He looked fondly at the dusty spot in the dirt. Sarah had two bunches of his flannel shirt in her fists. She pulled down on them so that her father had to look at her.

He looked at her for a long time. Then he put his palm on her forehead and pushed back, but not hard. She let go, and he walked over to the side of the van. My mother had already gotten in and started up. She rolled down the window.

"Now, you wouldn't be able to fix that little box there so I could get more channels, would ya?" I could smell his sour breath all the way in the backseat, and I marveled at the fact that my mother didn't make a face.

"Could I? Yes. Would I? No."

He shook his head, laughing to himself and kicking my mother's tire.

"It's not true about me losin' her, you hear?" He pulled his daughter close, crushed her to him like they were the best of pals.

"No sir," Sarah said, beaming up at him. She knew what he was going to say even before he said it. She was smiling because she knew he'd given in.

Mr. Kervick put his elbow in the van, leaned right over the open window, and said in a low voice to my mother, "Don't really matter what I say, 'cause that girl's gonna do what she's gonna do. Been that way since she was born."

"But it matters to me," my mother said. "And I'm *doing* here, too."

"There's nothin' more to it? I got your word?"

"You have my word," my mother said.

And he reached his hand into the car and she shook it.

As we were driving away, she said, "Now, I wonder what Sarah meant when she said you weren't afraid of everything. Is there a single thing you couldn't turn into a fatal accident? In fact, while Sarah's old man was making up his mind, I was amusing myself with all the tragic catastrophes you could make out of his place. Really. Lockjaw, Lyme disease, fatal spills, dog bites, hantavirus, West Nile, lung cancer . . ."

But I barely heard her. Even my phone call to Gloria was forgotten in the wake of that hair-raising experience. As my own fear slowly receded, I realized I had discovered something very interesting during that trip, and I wanted to think more about it. I had discovered what Sarah was afraid of. Even more than her daddy's swing, Sarah Kervick was afraid that someone would laugh at her dream.

CHAPTER EIGHT

Mrs. Boardman Breaks a Rule

Me: Gloria, you will never guess where I've been.

Gloria (*sounding tired*): Oh, hello, Franklin.

Me: Think rabid dogs, think insect-borne diseases . . .

Gloria: Don't tell me. You went to a pet store.

Me: Is anything wrong, Gloria? You sound like . . . well . . . not like yourself.

Gloria: Not my usual self, you mean? Well, now that you mention it, not every day at the National Safety Department is a good one. The terrible accidents, you can't imagine, Franklin. I don't suppose you're calling to cheer me up, are you?

Me (*unsure what to say next. It was Gloria's job to cheer me up, not the other way around*): I . . . uh . . .

Gloria: Tell me, Franklin. How is your friend? The one you're teaching to read?

Me: You mean Sarah Kervick.

Gloria: Yes, I think so. Sarah. Have you made any progress?

Me: That's where I was yesterday! She has two vicious dogs, Gloria. They actually attacked my mother's van. One of them nearly came inside, where I was imprisoned by my shoulder harness.

Gloria: I was talking about the girl, Franklin. Not the dogs, and *not you*.

Me: Oh, all right. Um . . . (*And since I hadn't made any*

progress on teaching Sarah to read, since I hadn't even really thought about it, I told Gloria everything else I knew about Sarah, about her new job, about the trailer where she lived, about her dream of being a figure skater, even the story about Sarah falling through the ice, which I decided would interest her professionally, seeing as drowning is the number-two accidental way for children to die.)

Gloria: She wants to be a figure skater, you say? That's an expensive sport, I'm afraid.

Me: And a dangerous one. I, for one, fail to see how figure skating differs significantly from rollerblading or skateboarding. And yet, protective headgear is not required in any of the competitive ice skating sports.

Gloria: Can't you see, Franklin? This goes way beyond a question of safety. It's about a dream. Having a dream and believing in the possibility of that dream coming true is what gives people hope. Hope is a much greater determinant of whether or not a person will survive and thrive than safety helmets. (*On this last line, Gloria raised her voice. I think it is safe to say she was shouting at me.*)

Me: I was merely pointing out that—

Gloria: I know, I know, Franklin, but honestly, sometimes you can't see the forest for the trees. When you get back to your reading, I want you to find the story of Pandora. It's a Greek myth. That story hasn't got anything to do with statistics, but it will certainly teach you a thing or two about life.

Me: I'd be happy to look up the story, Gloria, if you think that's a good idea. I just don't see—

Gloria: Franklin, would you say that this friend of

yours . . . Sarah . . . would you say that she has the means to pursue this dream of hers?

Me: Means?

Gloria: The money.

Me: Well, judging from the fact that up until my mother came into the picture she was not adequately clothed, I would say no, Gloria. I don't think Sarah Kervick has money to spare.

Gloria: Franklin! (*long pause*) I believe you have cheered me up (*sounding really happy now . . . I was totally confused*).

Me: I'm so glad, Gloria, that I could be of service.

Gloria: I made a promise to myself a long time ago that I would repay a debt, and I think I know now how I'm going to do that.

Me: Well, that's wonderful, Gloria. I know that one's financial picture can cause a lot of stress. Speaking of stress, my teacher, Ms. Linski, has signed me up to be in the Presidential Fitness Program along with the rest of our class, and one of the requirements is that we touch our toes. With my short arm and long leg, I'm afraid I won't be able to—

Gloria: Would you have any idea what her shoe size is, Franklin? Just off the top of your head?

Me: Off the top of my head? No, I wouldn't, Gloria. What does Sarah Kervick's shoe size have to do with—

Gloria: You must promise to get back to me on that. You can . . . Well, you can predict a great deal about . . . the future health of a person—longevity and so forth—from the size of her feet. Will you promise to get that for me, Franklin? Will you?

Me: You never asked for my foot size, Gloria.

Gloria: No, I haven't. But then, it's never been necessary, Franklin. You supply me with information about your health in agonizing detail.

As I hung up the phone, I realized that something had come between me and Gloria. And that something was Sarah Kervick.

But it seemed that the only way to get back into Gloria's good graces was to teach the girl to read. Even though I'd rather walk barefoot down the driveway or chew gum with artificial colors, I knew the task that lay before me.

And good old Mrs. Boardman was going to help.

In order to get Sarah alone, I decided I would just have to give up the health-promoting benefits of fresh air for a while. So I convinced Ms. Linski that my delicate physical state was best maintained in the library over lunchtime (besides that, I also promised to do a little extra-credit work hunting down cereal box toys on the Internet). She agreed—rather quickly, I might add—that we could give it a trial period. "But if you grow too pale, Franklin, it's back out in the sunshine."

I didn't make any moves at first, just let lunchtime in the library with Mrs. Boardman take on its own routine. Sarah put up with me, but I was to keep my mouth shut. Which I did for a while, knowing that if I sprung this idea right away, Sarah would banish me from the library altogether.

Those days were just as pleasant as the first one had been. First, Sarah and Mrs. Boardman talked, then Mrs. Boardman pulled something glossy out of her library bag. Then Sarah looked at the pictures. I just relaxed and read and enjoyed the reprieve from the playground.

After exactly ten days, I got quietly up from my assigned seat and approached the circulation desk.

"I'm interested in a Greek myth about somebody named Pandora," I told Mrs. Boardman. "Can you help me?"

Mrs. Boardman glanced up at me and smiled. Somewhere along the line, I'd crossed over from being one of those annoying kids who caused her to reshelve the books to someone she could stand having around. Swiveling around in her chair, she pulled out a book from the reference shelf and set it on the desk in front of her. The thick, dark green cover contained a picture of a man with wings sprouting out of his head. Underneath that were the words *Bulfinch's Mythology*.

The middle drawer of her desk squeaked open, and Mrs. Boardman pulled out a little rubber cap that she stretched over her index finger. She opened the book and carefully turned the pages, smoothing down each one as she went. Her bony wrists bent precariously as she handed me the heavy volume.

"Thank you," I whispered, and took it from her, walking directly over to Sarah, who lay on her stomach in the picture book section, poring over her latest skating book. I set the book directly onto a picture of a girl who seemed to be hanging in the air with her legs spread out at dangerous angles.

"What?" Sarah looked up at me, annoyed.

"My friend Gloria says you need to read this," I told her.

Sarah squinted at the small print before pulling her own book from beneath the one I'd set down. Then she shifted her position so she was over the pictures again.

"I'm serious," I said, staying where I was.

Sarah glared at me and flipped over the cover of the book so she could see the title.

"So read it," she said, as if it didn't really matter.

So I read her the story of Pandora, the girl who was sent to earth by the gods. She was the very first girl and every god and goddess did something to make her perfect. Then they sent her to earth to live with a guy named Epimetheus. In his house, Epimetheus had this box that he told Pandora she should never, under any circumstances, open. She did, of course. She couldn't control her curiosity. And out of the box came every bad thing that could ever happen to a person: sickness, poison, arthritis, old age, deformity. Those were just the diseases of the body. Then came the diseases of the mind, like sadness, jealousy, and despair.

Pandora was knocked flat by all these bad things rushing to get out and do their work in the world. She thought the box was empty, but at the bottom there was this little winged creature. She was Hope.

When I was finished, I glanced up at Sarah, who was resting her chin on her hands, listening.

"Read that last part again," she said. "The part about the evils."

" 'So we see at this day, whatever evils are abroad, hope never entirely leaves us; and while we have *that*, no amount of other ills can make us completely wretched.' "

Rolling over on her back, Sarah Kervick stared at the ceiling.

"Who's Gloria?" she said after a while.

"You can't read, can you?"

"Course I can read."

"You can't read much, then."

"Never was taught, was I? Didn't even go to school till I was eight."

"Well, if you want to be regular, you're going to have to learn to read."

Sarah reached up and yanked the fabric of my shirt so I lost my balance and hit the floor, shoulder first. There was no doubt this kind of collision would cause bruising.

"You think I don't know that?" she said.

"How come you don't ask for help, then? Or go to Coach Jablonski's class?"

"Lookin' like a retard, gettin' pulled out for special ed . . . you think that's regular?"

"I didn't know you had a choice." We were whispering, our faces so close to each other that a little bit of Sarah Kervick's spit landed on my cheek.

She grinned at me like she always did, without showing her teeth. "Can't test me, can they? Dad won't sign the papers."

"And you think you can pull that off forever?"

"That's how my dad did it."

It was on the tip of my tongue to mention that her dad hadn't exactly reached the pinnacle of success with this method. But I'd already been Sarah-handled once that afternoon.

"Aren't you just a little curious?" I asked her, changing my tactic. "Don't you want to know how to do this?" With my injured arm, I managed to push her skating book so that it faced us both.

"You can't just look at the pictures, see. It says here, 'It is essential to keep your weight over the left foot as you lead into the jump. With your right foot approximately twenty-four inches—'"

Sarah Kervick's palm slapped down on the picture with such strength that even slightly deaf Mrs. Boardman looked our way. Sitting up, she jammed her fists under her armpits.

"Course I want to know that." And her eyes started blinking so funny and her jaw was clenched and she didn't say any more, not for a long time.

And I figured something out then. Sarah wanted to learn to read better, but you can't go around threatening Coach Jablonski behind the school, now, can you? She just couldn't figure out a way to make it happen.

This was a day I never thought I'd see. In my six-year history at Pelican View Elementary, I had never seen Mrs. Boardman break a rule. She wouldn't even loan you one of the library's pencils if you forgot yours—which, actually, was never a problem for me, but one that Marvin Howerton seemed to have with regularity.

But that day, when I asked her for help, Mrs. Boardman gave me six(!) easy readers to check out. And when I whispered to her that we'd have to find some way to disguise them, she found a backpack at the bottom of the lost and found box.

"Things should be put to use," she said. "It's been here well over a year."

I handed the backpack to Sarah and told her, "Well, it's got to be after baseball practice. And don't pretend you're busy."

She clapped her arm around my shoulder and said, "Thanks, Donuthead."

And I said, "Don't mention it."

Later, I recalled with shock that I hadn't even checked her hand for warts.

A Historic Day

If my memory serves me correctly, it was about this same time that I learned my mother was receiving anonymous gifts. Not that she volunteered this information, mind you. I had to pry it out of her.

She was going on what looked suspiciously like a date with Paul, whom she'd met when she and her friend Penny—the animal lover with the unhygienic potluck dishes—had gone out one night to snicker at the karaoke singers at Z's Bar and Grille. Paul was one of them, but when he crooned the line "You can't escape my love," my mother punched Penny in the shoulder to shut her up.

"He's not so bad," she said.

"In more ways than one," Penny agreed.

She and Paul were only *friends*, she assured me. "No need to start grilling him yet, Franklin. We'll probably never cross the line. I don't really go for guys like Paul." But she'd get a dreamy look when she talked about him that put me on my guard.

On the evening in question, they were meeting friends and going to a movie. Afterwards, Paul might take the mike at a new karaoke bar in Brownfield.

As soon as my mother emerged from the bathroom, I planned to engage her in a lengthy discussion of the perils of leaving a child my age home alone after midnight, but I was temporarily overcome by the odor she gave off.

"Mother," I said, covering my mouth with the fabric of my T-shirt, "need I remind you of the effects of perfume on people with multiple chemical sensitivities?"

"Hold your nose, Franklin," she said, stuffing her wallet into a purse she used only when she went out on dates with men. "I'll be out of here in a sec."

In went car keys, Chap Stick, Dentyne. This was not looking good.

"How could you buy perfume? You know I'm allergic."

"I didn't buy it, for your information. It was a gift."

That's when the story came out. Gifts had been coming her way for a couple of weeks now. First, a dented package of snacks on the driver's seat of her van. Then her benefactor began leaving old copies of *People* magazine for her at work. Finally, she'd received this bottle of perfume on the back doorstep.

"That's it," I said. "We're calling the police."

"Whatever for, Franklin?"

I felt a headache the size of Texas crawling up my right shoulder.

"You're being stalked, Mother, and you're too innocent to know it."

"Stalked with *People* magazines? Get a grip."

The doorbell rang, and I vowed we'd continue this conversation later. Honestly, without me to look out for her, my mother was a walking time bomb.

"Just answer one question," I gasped, eyeing Paul suspiciously as he held the door for her. "Did you eat any of the food you were given?"

"Of course I ate it," she said. "Those Twinkies were still in the package. Now relax, Franklin. I'm your mother, not the other way around."

In April, we practiced baseball. I applied myself as well as I could, given my physical limitations. By the second week, I no longer ran away from the ball. By the third week, I stopped dropping the bat. Now, that's what I call progress.

Still, my mother had the habit of pulling off her baseball cap and wiping her forearm across her forehead, the way the major league coaches did.

When it was Sarah's turn, I trotted to the outfield and squinted into the sun. I guess my mother had forgotten our original purpose, which was to give me enough confidence to sign up for the Pelican View Baseball Team. Now she coached Sarah, too. In fact, I would say that Sarah was the only one she coached. For me, it was more about showing up.

I mostly just watched the practice happen at that point, jogging to the ball after it was hit. After all, you can't expect a kid with my physical limitations to play the positions of three able-bodied men. That's a lot of uneven ground to cover.

It was during that time I discovered my hidden talent. My mother says that most of my talents are hidden, but this one stayed hidden on purpose for quite a long while. If Sarah Kervick hadn't been such a hit parade, I might never have discovered the little secret that would make me feel special.

Even when my mother threw her trademark fast curve,

Sarah could whack the stuffing out of the baseball. More than strength, that girl had perfect placement and timing. You see, a batter can never know how a pitch will come in, or even whether or not she's standing at the right angle to meet it. So her reflexes have to be lightning fast. You had to watch closely, but you could see Sarah adjust her stance as the ball was coming in.

Of course, this made it hard to tell where the ball would be hit, but I almost always knew. That was my talent, certainly not as dramatic as hers, but one that fit the scientific workings of my mind. I could predict, with a statistical accuracy that would make Gloria Nelots send out recruiters, where that ball was headed. The fact that I arrived there too late to catch it was purely an act of self-defense. My weak wrists needed protection almost as much as my foreshortened arm and leg.

There's no mystery to where the runner goes after the ball is hit. The thing I couldn't figure out was how Sarah managed to work up so much speed so quickly. On that first day of practice, my mother had measured her footprint from a wet, sandy sample in the infield. After that, Sarah got cleats *and* tennis shoes. With the traction she got from the cleats, she sped around the bases like liquid fire, dirt spitting from the bottoms of her feet and her blond hair flying behind her like the tail of a kite.

By the end of April, Sarah had a baseball jacket, two pairs of jeans, and three regular-looking girl shirts. Her hair was combed, her warts were all but gone, and she'd graduated to second-grade readers. Just walking down the street, someone would definitely mistake her for regular.

After we got home from practice, my mother would make

Sarah a monstrous snack. Thick slices of salami and cheese and lettuce and tomato on huge slabs of bread. It's hard to imagine how she got her mouth around it. I was tempted to point out that swallowing without chewing was putting an unnecessary burden on her digestive tract, not to mention what all the added dyes, fillers, and preservatives were doing to her health profile. But I knew that Sarah would only laugh at me with her mouth open, flicking bits of sausage onto my snack of dry roasted soybeans and unsalted pumpkin seeds.

"You know, Franklin, I got a question for you," she said one day after inhaling two beef tacos and an entire can of pears in heavy syrup. "You're always trying to eat so healthy and not get hurt. How come?"

"You're asking me why I try to avoid risky behaviors? Why I try to eat a healthy balance of foods?"

"Sure," she said, pouring juice from the can onto her spoon and slurping it. "How come?"

"Well, I think it would be obvious to even the most casual observer that my health is not robust," I responded.

"You know a lotta big words, Franklin, but I still don't get it. I mean . . . I know why I do what I do. I do the baseball thing 'cause I get clothes and that makes me look regular. And I read these stupid books about frogs losin' buttons and a bunch of stupid crap that would bore a two-year-old so that someday I can read the stuff in those skating books.

"But as far as I can tell, the only thing that gets you goin' is how sick you are and how deformed you are and all that, so I figure you oughta stick your head in the path of a speeding pitch and get beaned. Then you could spend a coupla weeks in the hospital hooked up to those machines and talk all day to the doctors and nurses about how sick you are."

"Well," I said, re-capping my yogurt. "Well."

The truth was, I'd never heard Sarah Kervick talk so much. It never occurred to me that she even thought about me, let alone thought about ways to occupy my time.

I liked it and I didn't like it. I mean, I liked the attention, but I didn't like what it all added up to. As she sat there slurping her syrup, I realized that Sarah Kervick had decided I was in this for reasons other than a sterling bill of health. That I had needs, emotional needs, that caused me to act in certain ways. I was about to correct her on several points when I decided I just didn't want to be in the same room with Sarah Kervick right then. What I decided was that two of us could play at this case-study business. How would she feel, I wondered, to be the object of such unflattering scrutiny?

"I need to make a phone call," I said. "Then we'll get started."

Gloria wasn't in. She was testifying before the Senate Sub-committee on Food and Drug Packaging, according to her assistant, Miss Tweedell.

"Problem is, kids can't get into those childproof pill bottles, but neither can old people, now can they?" she asked, apparently without expecting an answer. "Want her voice mail?"

"Sure," I said, walking over to the front door and picking up one of Sarah's sandy tennis shoes. I'd never left a message for Gloria before. I cleared my throat and got ready to enunciate.

"Gloria, I got that information you wanted. Sarah Kervick wears a size six shoe. She's around four feet, ten inches tall, and she can't weigh more than seventy pounds. A couple of her teeth are brown, and her father smokes." I paused, wondering if there was anything more I could add to get into Gloria's good graces, and to show that I was thinking of someone other than myself. "She lives in a trailer off a dirt road," I ended. Then I hung up the phone, went to my room, and shut the door.

Sarah could practice *Frog and Toad Are Friends* on her own today.

The Pelican View Baseball Team had its first meeting April 30. All the kids who wanted to be on the team were there, along with their parents. My mother was doing double duty, bringing me and Sarah to the practice.

"Franklin," Coach Jablonski said, all jovial, slapping me on the back and bruising my deltoid muscle. "This is a surprise. And you brought your lady friend." At this he winked.

"You know, dear, the cheerleaders are with Miss Debby in the multipurpose room."

"She's here for the baseball meeting," my mother said, stepping forward. "Hello, Hank."

"Well, hey, Julia. The baseball team. Well . . ." He looked skinny old Sarah Kervick up and down. "It's just . . ." Squinting his eyes, Coach Jablonski peered around the bleachers. "She might get lonely, is all. Girls' softball, that's in the fall."

"No trouble about that," Sarah said, bruising my other deltoid with a solid slap. "I got Franklin here."

Marvin Howerton opened his mouth, but then thought better of it.

When it was time to start, Coach Jablonski blew a couple of

short bleeps on his whistle and slapped his clipboard against his thigh.

"Good news, sports fans. The Pelican View Ice and Fitness Center is having its grand opening next month. Now, as many of you know, I played wing for Loggertown State, and I look forward to being the coach of the first ever Pelican View Hockey Team. So I want all of you to think about taking my basic skills class this summer."

He looked around, as if expecting us to say something, but nobody did.

"Well," he said, clearing his throat. "Just thought I'd give you a preview of coming attractions. Now let's play ball. Can I have a parent volunteer to pitch for batting practice?"

Marvin Howerton's father, who looked just like Marvin only super-sized, stepped forward. So did my mother.

"Thanks, Jim," Coach Jablonski said. "That'll be all. The rest of you can take a seat in the bleachers. I've got the health forms all ready on clipboards for you to sign."

Another few bleeps on the whistle, even though no one was talking. I was tempted to ask if Coach knew the decibel level of his whistle blasts, but I changed my mind. It was better not to draw attention to myself.

"Count off," he roared.

There were only seventeen kids total who signed up for the privilege of playing on the Pelican View Baseball Team. All the really good athletes joined Little League, I guess. I felt a brief and intense sense of gratitude that this thought had not yet occurred to my mother.

Luckily, I turned out to be a two. We were to take the field.

I ambled toward right, glancing back at my mother, who was installed in the bleachers, looking disgusted.

Marvin Howerton was first up to bat. From his stance, I could tell the ball wouldn't come anywhere near me, so I could relax. Mr. Howerton pitched his son an easy lob, slow and level. If he hit the ball with proper force, I predicted it would crest the third base line, just over Graham Dewar's head.

But I underestimated Graham, who leapt into the air like a frog as soon as Marvin hit the ball and caught the drive squarely in his glove. Marvin pounded home plate with the bat, muttering.

"All right, boy," Mr. Howerton shouted. "It was a good hit."

Denny Price was up next. Mr. Howerton lobbed an easy one to Denny, who popped up to center field. We didn't have enough players to cover center, so Leonard Morris came flying in from left field to miss the catch and sprawl on the ground. Personally, I could have told him that he didn't have enough acceleration to make the catch. I did, if I'd started with the pitch, but why place myself in a dangerous spot for a practice session?

I began to limp painfully toward the ball, just to show I had a grasp on the rules of the game. Secretly, I was giving Leonard the opportunity to jump up, remember the direction of home plate, scoop up the ball, and fling it crazily toward Mr. Howerton, who had run in to cover.

After that, Mack Simmons grounded to short, sending Leonard flying forward. His heart rate must have been off the charts.

Now Sarah was up to bat, and I could see Mr. Howerton

change his pitching strategy. The ball came in fast and low on the inside, nearly clipping off Sarah's knees in the process. The second one sailed right past her nose. My mother practically climbed the backstop.

"Throw her a decent pitch, Jim. Or I'll relieve you," she shouted.

"Now, Julia. That'll be my decision," Coach Jablonski called out from the first base line.

"Like hell it will," she replied.

Sarah walked away from home plate and whispered something to my mother at the fence. For some reason it made me feel awfully lonely out there in right field, getting all these twinges in my legs from the uneven ground and watching, from a distance, my mother and Sarah Kervick with their heads together.

Before she returned to her stance, Sarah waved her bat at me.

That's when I knew she was headed in my direction. Instead of banging a hit to the ghost man in center field and streaming around the bases all triumphant, she was going to lob me an easy one. She didn't care how Mr. Howerton pitched. That was what she was going to do.

I could see her change her footing and lower her bat. All I needed to do was keep a cool head and place myself under the ball. So what if I got hit, I said to myself. The doctors in the hospital might finally confirm what I'd been telling my mother all along. Baseball was no kind of game for a sensitive, asymmetrical guy like me.

I predicted Mr. Howerton would pitch a strike. He did. But

it was low and fast. I had to move back quickly to reach the right spot. I began to backpedal, hoping that my mother was paying attention. Could she see the effort I was putting into this?

Breathing in little gasps, I was almost to the spot when I heard the thundering crack of the bat. It was at that exact moment that my short heel hit a rock. I lost my balance and careened toward the ground, stretching out my arms to cushion the blow. As I fell in a long, slow-motion arc that ended on hard-packed earth, I spied, out of the corner of my eye, crazy Leonard Morris. He'd been streaking over to back me up, but when I fell, he froze, his eyes following the trajectory of the ball like it was a meteor streaking toward earth.

I wish I could say it was a heroic dive to catch the ball, but I'm an honest guy. I bounced on the ground a couple of times before realizing it was coming straight at me. I threw my hands up to protect myself. There was nothing between me and that speeding bullet but a thin layer of cow skin. By some miracle it worked. The material held, and I took the fly on the ground.

I could hear my mother cheering and rattling the backstop.

"Way to go, Franklin," called out Leonard Morris.

Despite the fact that the tendons in my hand were sure to need months of physical therapy to recover, I have to admit, at that moment I felt pretty good.

CHAPTER TEN

Sarah Kervick Finds a Home

In addition to team practice twice a week and drills once a week, my mother drove me and Sarah Kervick all over the county scouting out the competition. We'd rattle up to some dusty field in her Cable Country van, get out, and take to the bleachers. Sarah didn't have much use for sitting. Mostly, she paced the baselines with my mother. But every once in a while, she'd sit up high in the bleachers with me.

I found watching to be the best part of joining the Pelican View Baseball Team. Every player I saw gave me greater opportunities to practice my newly discovered skill of knowing just exactly where the ball would be hit. Yes, I had to take into account several factors: speed of pitch, player's stance, level of swing. Then I'd process it all with the speed of nanotechnology. I've always preferred exercising my brain to my body anyway.

Honestly, I could get into quite a trance while I was watching those players. Sometimes I would forget all about Sarah and my mother and just enter this zone of processing impact, force, acceleration. That's why I was completely unprepared one afternoon for Sarah to turn to me and say, "So, where is your dad, anyway?"

"Haven't got one," I answered after a long pause.

"Everybody's got one." She snorted.

"Midcenter, pop fly. If the shortstop were back ten feet, he'd catch it," I said, thinking out loud so Sarah would know where my mind was. *On the game, not on the elements of human reproduction.*

"I said, 'Everybody's got one,' Franklin. Even you."

Taking a hint was not her specialty.

"Technically, that is correct. Grounding out down the first base line . . ."

"So where is he?"

"I don't know. We never met him."

"You're sayin' your mom never met your dad?"

"That is correct. Look at his shoulders. That kid's going to foul over the third base line." We both sat still, watching to see if my prediction came true. It did.

"You're lying to me."

"No, I'm not. Look, there's something called artificial insemination. When a woman wants a baby, but she doesn't have a partner, she can pay to get a man's sperm—"

"That's pure crazy to pay for that," she said. "All you have to do is go down to a bar and start buyin' drinks."

"That's how you came about? I think there's a little issue called quality control here."

Sarah Kervick grabbed hold of my lapels in a way she hadn't in a long time. "What are you saying about my mother? She married my dad good and proper. Only, it's just—" She broke her hold and sat back, sitting on her hands to keep them from tearing my neck off my shoulders.

"She was just too young," she said quietly.

"Well, at least you knew her," I responded, my feelings hurt as much as my collarbone.

"He didn't get like that till after," she said. "We even had a place over in Wing Rock, a little house. It was just one story, but it had a dormer upstairs and I slept there. I remember that house . . . when I was real little we lived there."

I kept my eyes on the field, but I had stopped seeing the action. I couldn't have called the next play if it was in slow motion.

"She took me to one of those shows at the arena. You know, where they tell a story on the ice. She loved to watch the skaters on TV.

" 'Look at her!' she used to say to my dad. 'That's as close as we humans are ever gonna get to flying.' "

Practice was over. My mother started climbing the bleachers toward us.

"My mom was all right," Sarah said, squinting fiercely at home plate, even though no one was up to bat. "She was just too young."

"So where is she now?" I asked. "You ever see her?"

"Hmmph." Sarah hunched up her shoulders. "I guess she lives in your dad's neighborhood now."

"Hey." My mother had reached us, slightly out of breath. She sat down next to Sarah and patted her knee. "I keep meaning to say thanks for the Twinkies. Vanilla's my favorite."

Sarah searched the empty space beneath the bleachers like she had dropped something. She was smiling.

"And everybody at work's been fighting over that *People* with the interviews of death row inmates who get married. That's just hard to figure."

"Yeah." Sarah swallowed and looked up at my mother like

she was the one thing that made sense in this crazy world. Like if she were a death row inmate, Sarah Kervick would marry her.

"Franklin, I'll just be a minute, okay? I want to find out what that coach has done to his pitcher. Did you see those strikes?"

The wind had picked up again. She zipped her warm-up suit right up to her chin, then put her hand back on Sarah's knee. "A month ago, at the beginning of the season, that kid couldn't even find the strike zone. Okay, then. See you two back at the car."

"I know what you're thinkin'," Sarah said after she'd left. "But I didn't steal anything. Your mom wouldn't like that."

"Well, where's it all come from?"

"Grace gives me the magazines when the library in Wing Rock's through with 'em," she said simply.

"And the perfume?"

"Found it in the bathroom at Megamart."

I started to feel faint. "And the food?"

"Get that from the garbage at school. Kids throw that stuff away. Perfectly good Twinkies and stuff. They just throw the whole thing away, right in the package. I got four of those little cans of peaches to give her next week."

And then she laughed and gave me a little punch on the arm. "Don't look like you're gonna die, Franklin. I never take stuff that's been opened. Same as gettin' it right from the grocery store." She patted my knee as if that would make me feel better. "Only it's not stealin' and I don't have to pay for it."

I just stared at her, speechless. All this touching was getting contagious.

These new developments, the touching and the gifts, were

going to need a lot of processing. But I have to admit, the first question that popped into my mind was a very uncharacteristic one:

What was so wrong with it?

Giving things to people who made you feel happy. It was like one big circle with Sarah Kervick and my mother. One big circle filled with Twinkies and cream rinse and low-rise jeans and wrinkled-up copies of *People* magazine.

It made everybody even happier, didn't it?

Why wasn't I happy, then? Why was I so sick with jealousy at the way Sarah looked at my mother? Maybe I should get in the circle and start doling out Baby Ruth candy bars and sparkly barrettes and Jean Naté perfume and jawbreakers I might find rolling under the candy dispenser.

Maybe . . . Was that really all it took?

On the way home, my mother swung into the parking lot of an immense new building. Workers out front were lowering trees into the ground. On an artificial hill topped with wood chips, a sign read: PELICAN VIEW ICE AND FITNESS CENTER.

"So, what's this?" Sarah asked, squinting at the sign.

"You can read that," I told her.

"The new ice rink," my mother said, craning her head around to see the reaction. "Thought you'd like to take a look."

Sarah gripped the door handle and her seat belt simultaneously. The next moment, she was tearing for the entrance.

"Whoa, missy. Hold up. It's not open yet." A man in a hard hat stood just outside the glass front doors, smoking a cigarette.

"She's with me," my mother said.

"Oh." He took in her uniform. "You here to hook up the office?"

"Just seein' what I need first. Got the kids with me."

"Office is through those double doors," he said, pointing. "Hang a right. Mind the paint."

"Shouldn't we ask for masks?" I wondered aloud. Painting releases all manner of volatile compounds into the air.

But no one seemed to hear me. We entered a wide corridor where workers were installing a bank of vending machines. Beyond that was a sports shop. A woman was putting the finishing touches on a mannequin. I stopped to look at her handiwork, transfixed.

There in front of me was the most complete set of protective gear I'd ever seen. Every muscle, every inch of skin seemed to be covered. A helmet with a cage over the face was connected to a chin guard that extended down to protect the neck and throat area. Wide plastic gloves like flippers traveled halfway up the arms. There was sufficient padding for the midsection and thighs and practically a knight's shield to cover each lower leg.

"Get a move on," Sarah hissed. "I want to see the rink."

"It's a goalie's uniform, Franklin," my mother said, gently taking hold of my shoulders and turning me toward the office.

"It's a thing of beauty," I mumbled. "Do they have something like this for baseball?"

But my mother didn't hear me because I had my mouth up against the fabric of my shirt, trying to filter out the fumes from the new paint.

We continued down the hall and through another set of

double doors. The entire area was carpeted with the kind of rubber matting that seemed appropriate for all indoor office environments, if you ask me.

"This is so you can walk in your skates," my mother explained. "See, you change into your skates here," she said, pointing to a row of benches with cubicles underneath. "You stick your shoes there. Then you don't damage your blades getting to the rink."

"That's real sensible," Sarah answered, nodding. But she seemed a million miles away just then. I was watching her. Her eyes were fixed on another set of doors.

"Is it there?" she said.

"Yes."

She started walking slowly toward the doors.

"But it's not an ice rink yet," my mother warned her. "It's just a big oval that . . ." Her voice trailed off. There was no use talking anymore. Sarah disappeared through the swinging doors.

"Just give me a minute, Franklin. I need to see how they've wired the office so I can figure out how much cable I need."

She disappeared, too, and I was left alone in the hallway. My sinuses were throbbing from the fumes, but since I'm also allergic to dust and pollen, and those earth-moving machines were operating with decibel levels unsafe without proper ear protection, I wandered back down the hall to the goalie uniform.

Who was the packaging expert that put this together? My eyes traveled the length of the player's body, looking for openings in his armor. This would definitely have applications on the Pelican View playground.

"Franklin." My mother had poked her head through the door. "I think you should see this."

"That your kid?" a man in a paint-spattered coverall asked my mother as I came back into the room. He wasn't referring to me. That was clear. He was pointing to the windows above the changing benches.

"Yeah . . . well, I brought her."

"Seemed so excited I didn't have the heart to tell her there wasn't no ice yet," he said.

I stood up on one of the changing benches to get a clearer look at what the painter and my mother were staring at.

"Then again, doesn't seem to matter, does it?"

There, in the middle of an immaculate, glassy oval, stood Sarah Kervick, her discarded shoes the only other spot of color on the clean white surface.

Throwing her arms out to her sides, she began to twirl. Slowly, at first, and then faster and faster. If she kept it up, she was headed for a fall.

"That looks like glass," I said to the painter. "What kind of cushioning have they installed beneath the surface?"

"Beats me, kid." He shrugged, his eyes glued on Sarah.

"For heaven's sake, Franklin. I didn't call you over here to assess the hazards of what she's doing. Look at her face."

Only Sarah Kervick could find a way to look relaxed as she twirled dangerously over that slippery surface. Her eyes were closed like she was in a trance, and her body was all limp and fluid, not like the way she usually held herself, rigid as a flagpole.

"She looks like a little angel out there," the painter said, sighing. "A pretty little angel."

"I've never seen her so at home," my mother said softly.

The paint fumes in that place must have been very bad, because my mother started rubbing her eyes.

You could hardly stand there for long without your eyes watering.

CHAPTER ELEVEN

Sarah Kervick's Show-Stopping Hit

If you experience something every day, it gets to be normal, even when it's not. In Pelican View, few things are considered normal, which might lead you to believe it's kind of a crazy place. That's not it at all. The goal seemed to be to push everyone and everything into that narrow band of what was considered normal. People figured if they worked on it long enough, just about everyone would either fit or pick up and move away.

By now, it should be pretty clear that I was not normal. And neither was Sarah Kervick.

She was especially not normal on the baseball diamond.

I don't care how many girls have been the prime minister of England. In Pelican View, girls did not play baseball.

But that's what I mean about force of habit. After a couple of weeks of practice, having Sarah on the team *did* become normal, even to Coach Jablonski. She came to every practice. She consistently hit over the infielders' heads. It was no surprise to me to read on our first game roster that Sarah Kervick was batting cleanup.

Marvin Howerton could not let this pass, however. He scuffed at the ground and whined, "You got a girl batting cleanup?"

"I got our best batter at cleanup," Coach Jablonski said,

putting his hands on Marvin's shoulders. "You get on base and let her boot you in."

I had to turn the batting roster over to find my name, which gave me some hope that I might not see active duty in this game. I would have appreciated at least one game to get used to wearing the team uniform. My skin is very sensitive and, as a result, I have a strict policy about natural fibers. But our baseball uniforms, purchased by Modern Hardware, our team sponsor, came only in a polyester blend. I had on a long-sleeved 100 percent organic cotton T-shirt, but this did nothing for my thighs.

Of course, my mother had to use up three rolls of film snapping pictures of me in my uniform, as well as crouched in my batting stance.

"Grimace a little," she'd said. "This could be our Christmas card."

The other team was from Brownfield Elementary. They were sponsored by Z's Bar and Grille. Not particularly talented, the team had a couple of solid hitters. They weren't fast and they weren't polite. That's what I'd picked up from watching them practice.

We were up first. Graham popped up and Leonard grounded out, so we were already two down by the time Marvin got up to bat. He hit a nice double between short and second base.

I guess there really are some good things about being on a team. I bet Marvin Howerton never thought one nice thing about Sarah up until that moment. But as he sat there on second base, the desire to be the first to score in the very first game of the season for Pelican View Elementary's Modern Hardware Team had him thinking positive thoughts about her.

Come to think of it, maybe that's what jinxed her.

"You got a girl? Batting cleanup?" the pitcher asked to no one in particular.

"You got a problem with that?" Sarah asked, advancing toward the mound.

He held up his glove and tiptoed backward, pretending to be afraid of her. "No problem there. I just hope I don't hit you anywhere sensitive, is all."

Sarah would have clocked him, but my mother was on the field by this time, talking her down. I felt pretty confident that she would not clock my mother, who at this moment, I would just bet, was telling Sarah that famous Franklin Delano Roosevelt line "If you treat people right, they will treat you right."

Of course, she might have left off the last part. FDR was an optimist, not a dummy. The last part of that quote was "ninety percent of the time."

When Sarah got back in her stance, I knew something was wrong.

The thing about Sarah Kervick is she's so flexible and wiry. Like her punch that seems to come from nowhere, she doesn't have to hold a bat just right to knock the ball out of the park. It's just instinct.

But now she was in position with her bat cocked just so. All of a sudden, she cared. I knew that was dangerous.

On the first swing, her timing was off. On the second, she swung like a girl, in a high arc that looked more like a dance step than a batter's move. On the third, she'd already accepted defeat. She slouched back to the bench and didn't even turn around when the pitcher said some rotten thing about girls being good at cleaning up, he just wasn't sure that meant baseball.

I can't tell you how I felt right then, but "pure lousy," as Sarah would say, comes pretty close. The things you knew about Sarah Kervick were that, yes, she had a dad swinging at her and she lived in a dirty old trailer. She didn't have two dimes to rub together, but that girl was going to end up okay. She had this way of persuading people. Okay, so maybe it was a little prehistoric, but knowing that last thing about the girl made you feel better about the first things.

"Girls can't take the pressure," Marvin said to Leonard as they got their gloves.

I thought she was going to clean his clock. I thought she was going to make his lungs exchange places. But Sarah just shrugged and sat on the bench. I handed over her glove.

"I'm not goin'," she said. "I'm tired."

"You gotta go out there. You're the mighty vacuum of the left field. You're the black hole. Every ball that will be hit this season will be magnetically attracted to your glove," I said.

"Forget it, Franklin. I said I'm tired." She said that a little mean, pressing her lips into a frown. Even I wasn't afraid of her.

"You're gonna let that lousy pitcher get the best of you? Come on, you're more than that."

She shifted away from me and started pulling splinters off the bench. I knew it was time to say something right. I knew it was time to give that important speech that they give in movies, the one that turns everything around. But I'm good only at a couple of things and making speeches isn't one of them.

"Are we a team?" I asked, thumping my chest just like Franklin Delano Roosevelt. I had to resist the urge to look under my shirt to see if I'd produced a bruise.

Instead I blurted out, "Happiness lies in the joy of achievement," which was the only FDR quote I could think of at the moment.

Except for a little spittle on her hair, I was having no effect on Sarah Kervick.

"We're the greatest, remember? Kervick and Donuthead. Your arms and my eyes. Our secret weapon."

"Yeah, they're gonna write about it in the newspaper," she mumbled.

"You're the greatest vacuum in the history of Pelican View Elementary, and I'm going to show you where the dirt is!"

I was hopping up and down at this point.

Sarah Kervick gave me a long, slow look. She wiped a little spit off her face and said, "Are you okay, Franklin? Maybe you better sit down."

Coach Jablonski came sweeping along the bench. "Get out there, Kervick," he shouted from close range. "Shake it off."

"Get out there, Kervick," I shouted for effect. "And keep your eyes on me."

So Sarah took the field and I stood along the third base line.

And by some miracle she did decide to keep her eyes on me.

On the first play I waved her in, right behind the second baseman. She caught the lazy fly easily.

The second play was going to right field. Bryce Jordan was

playing too far back, but I had no way of telling him that. The ball dribbled into the outfield between first and second. I consoled myself with the knowledge that Bryce didn't have the arm to make the play anyway.

Luis got wild on the mound and walked the third guy, which wasn't a bad decision because he was a switch-hitter and those were hard for me to judge.

What do you know? The pitcher was batting cleanup. In the pros, the pitcher never bats cleanup. Pitchers are notoriously bad at the plate.

Never say never, Franklin. I sent Sarah Kervick to the horizon before he'd even cocked his elbow. This guy could hit. She was at the fence, twirling a piece of her long blond hair, when she took the catch.

The guy on first base made the mistake of thinking that Sarah Kervick threw like a girl. He almost lost an ear as she fired it back to second. Three down.

"I don't know how she does it," Coach Jablonski said, rubbing his stomach in admiration. "That girl always knows where the ball's gonna be."

"It's practice, Hank," my mother said. "Hours and hours of fine-tuning in practice."

The bottom of the order had to come sometime. Top of the third. Pelican View leading, 1–0. The only good thing about going up to bat was knowing that Sarah Kervick would soon follow. Now that she'd loosened up a bit, she was going to show them what for, she was going to show them what little girls are made of, I thought, practicing in my mind the inspirational speech I was going to send her to the plate with.

But first, I had to make the long, lonely walk to the on-deck circle myself.

I decided to spend my time choosing a bat rather than practicing my swing. I didn't want to give the other team a preview of what I could do.

It's all mental, I told myself to quiet the shivering. *Let 'em think I'm the Pelican View Elementary secret weapon.*

It's true, I have a pretty active imagination, and if people can go into a trance and walk over beds of burning coals, I should, theoretically, be able to convince myself to get a single for Modern Hardware and my teammates on the Pelican View Baseball Team.

Unfortunately, imagination can work two ways.

As I stood facing the pitcher, I realized that this was not my mother, not Sarah Kervick, not even Coach Jablonski. This was the enemy about to fire a missile at me. And I, Franklin Delano Donuthead, was giving him a clear shot.

I froze.

The pitcher zinged in a strike at the rate of a speeding bullet. Some part of my brain told me to swing, but it must have been that part that nobody listens to. My feet grew roots.

Another strike fired by. The breeze gave me a chill.

I could hear my mother's distant voice screaming, "Swing, Franklin!"

"Snap out of it, kid," Sarah yelled to me. Even in my disordered state, I could tell it was more of a threat than a plea.

"Whatsa matter?" the pitcher asked, laughing. "He turn into a statue or somethin'?"

"Maybe I need to wind him up," the catcher said, and they laughed so hard the catcher started wheezing and the ump called time out so he could take a shot on his inhaler.

"Play ball," Coach Jablonski yelled from the sidelines.

The pitcher threw a crooked lob that bounced in the dirt.

"Maybe his batteries ran down," the catcher snickered as he scrambled for the ball.

Ha. Ha. Ha. Another wild pitch, this one blissfully wide. Ball two.

To make a long story mercifully short, I got on base because the pitcher couldn't stop laughing long enough to throw a third strike.

"Let's see if he moves," the catcher said, coming up behind me and giving me a shove.

As any orthopedic surgeon could tell you, my center of gravity is severely affected by the differing lengths of my legs, so it will come as no surprise that I stumbled and almost fell to the ground.

"Lay off, catcher," I heard Sarah Kervick threaten. I'd heard that tone of voice before.

Dazed, I trotted down the first base line, trying to console myself. After all, whether I got a hit or not was immaterial. Even FDR understood that. "I have no expectation of making a hit every time I come to bat," he told the American people as he was trying to rebuild the country after the Great Depression. "What I seek is the highest possible batting average, not only for myself, but for my team."

So there, Mr. Fancy-Pants Pitcher. I bet he didn't even know what the letters FDR stood for.

Upon reaching first base, I tried to tag up, but the gorilla who was guarding it kept shoving me away.

Sarah had followed me down the baseline. She stood, just a few feet away, watching this.

"Don't mess with him," she said, both hands clenched into fists at her sides.

"Whaddryou? His bodyguard?"

We were at the top of the order, and Milton Summers was up. But the focus of the game seemed to have shifted to first base.

"If I could be allowed to make a point here," I said, tapping the dough-colored bag at our feet. "The rules of the game stipulate that runners on base have one foot in contact with the base at all times—"

"But my rules say that when nobody's watching, I mess with runts like you."

"I'm watching," Sarah said quietly.

"Oh yeah? Then watch this." And he gave me a shove between my shoulder blades that sent me to the ground.

I believe I lost consciousness for a moment, because the next thing I knew the first baseman screamed, "I'm bleeding!"

"Fight!" someone called out. Then bodies piled on top of me and we were all squirming in the dirt.

"I'm hyperventilating," I screamed in agony. "I need oxygen!"

"Shut up and hit somebody, Franklin," Sarah Kervick growled. "It's a fight."

I threw up my arms to protect my face, and my fist came in contact with soft flesh.

"Ouch," came a muffled voice by my ear. "The runt gave me a shiner!"

Needless to say, Sarah Kervick did not get another chance to prove her abilities at the plate. But I doubt that anybody on the Z's Bar and Grille team walked away saying that the girl can't hit.

CHAPTER TWELVE

Strange People Who Do Wonderful Things

"After all that work, Sarah . . .

"This was your chance to show them what you're made of . . .

"If you can't learn to concentrate better than that . . ."

Blah, blah, blah. My mother was in fine lecturing form all the way home.

Sarah Kervick was quiet. She looked out the window at the blur of houses and trees and mailboxes and didn't say a word.

Not until my mother said she didn't work so hard just to have a kid turn out to be a bully, et cetera, did she get a reply.

"How come I have to do all the work? That's what I wanna know," Sarah muttered.

"What's that?" my mother said.

"He's your kid, right? You ever teach him any get back? My dad would have somethin' to say to that first baseman's dad. If my dad just stood there and took it while I was bein' shoved around, why, he'd be no dad at all to me."

She sank down in her seat then, folding her shoulders in toward her chest like that little speech had exhausted her.

My mother was silent.

"You've got a point there," she said finally.

I reached over and touched Sarah Kervick's cheek. She winced. A bruise was beginning to form.

"Are you okay?" I asked quietly.

"Don't think about it and it doesn't hurt," she responded.

"Thanks for sticking up for me," I said. "I'm not really used to it." *Though I could get used to it.*

"Don't mention it."

So I didn't mention it, or anything else, the rest of the way home. I just sat with the fact that I, Franklin Delano Donuthead, had participated in my first "base-brawl." Actively, mind you. I did deliver a shiner. I waited for my conscience to catch up with my principles and assault me with guilt. I waited for several miles. But it didn't happen.

Sarah's regular clothes and her backpack were at our house, so we swung by there first before taking her home. There was a package on the doorstep.

At first, I thought my eyes had been affected by the brawl. We all stood around gaping at the lettering. It was from the National Safety Department. And it was addressed to "Franklin's Friend, Sarah."

"It's for you," my mother said, breaking our astonished silence. "Do you want to open it here or wait until you get home?"

Sarah looked at me closely as if to ask what I was playing at.

I just shrugged my shoulders. Gloria had sent a package to my house and it wasn't for me. This day was not improving.

We went inside and put the package on the kitchen table. It was wrapped in creased brown grocery paper and tied several times with knots.

My mother pulled the utility knife from her pocket and looked at Sarah. "Okay?" she said.

"Whatever."

My mother cut the twine. Sarah opened the box to reveal another heavy cardboard box. There was a note taped to it. She looked at me.

"Go on," I said. "You can read it."

The first part was a poem by Langston Hughes. I'd read it before. It was called "Dreams." Sarah put her finger under the word and started to sound it out. "Dre-aims," she said.

"No, this is one of those words where you just hear the first vowel," I told her. She got it right on the second try.

"Okay," she said, squinting.

I made a mental note that we should get her eyes checked. Maybe she didn't just do that for effect.

Sarah Kervick started reading. She did pretty well. I was proud of her. That girl is a quick study.

> Hold fast to dreams
> For if dreams die
> Life is a broken-winged bird
> That cannot fly.
>
> Hold fast to dreams
> For when dreams go
> Life is a barren field
> Frozen with snow.

"That's real pretty," she said. "You read the rest now, Franklin."

• • •

Dear Sarah,

I had a dream once. My dream was to go to college, and when one of my teachers told her father about my dream, he made it possible. Imagine that. A complete stranger to me! The world is full of people like that. Strange people who do wonderful things.

Hold fast to your dream, Sarah. Wrap it, as Langston Hughes says, "in a blue-cloud cloth away from the too-rough fingers of the world." And surround yourself with people who believe in that dream for you. And you will achieve it.

Your friend,
Gloria Nelots
Gloria Nelots
Chief Statistician, National Safety Department

Carefully, Sarah lifted out the box and took off the lid. Lying there, in a bed of tissue, were two gleaming white figure skates. She took out one and cradled it in her arms like a baby. After she traced the curves with her fingers, Sarah Kervick replaced the first skate and did the very same thing to the other one.

She smoothed the tissue down over them and stepped away from the box. There was an unreadable look on her face as Sarah Kervick tried to put her whole fist in her mouth.

When she realized she wasn't alone in the room, Sarah mumbled something about having to use the bathroom. We heard the sound of the door slamming and then the faucet being turned on full blast. Then she got the shower running and flushed the toilet several times. But even above the sound of all that gushing water, we could still hear Sarah Kervick crying.

After that day, Sarah Kervick was a different girl. It used to be that she only relaxed at isolated moments. Like those ranks of soldiers you see in movies, she was at attention most of the time, just waiting for some general to smack her from behind. Zooming through the infield or looking at those step-by-step pictures of how to twirl on ice were the only times she was at ease.

Now she was relaxed more often. Her hands stopped balling into fists. She smiled and showed her teeth. Three days after Gloria sent her the skates, Sarah's father came to school. He had shaved and put on a clean shirt buttoned all the way up to his chin. Sarah was gone from the class for a long time, and Mr. Putman had a substitute sent in for Ms. Linski.

"I'll be goin' to the resource room now," she told me and Mrs. Boardman at lunchtime. "And we don't have to get in trouble or say we're sick or nothin' to come here, either."

She looked me up and down. "You're still gonna help me, right, Franklin?"

I swallowed and nodded yes.

"That's a relief. 'Cause the crap they give me to read is even more boring than the crap you give me."

"Gee, thanks," I replied.

But it made me feel a little sick the way she said it, because I knew right then that Sarah Kervick was feeling sorry for me. Pitying me and pounding on me were just about the only two ways fifth graders interacted with me at Pelican View Elementary. Up until then, Sarah Kervick had been the first person in recorded history to treat Franklin Delano Donuthead like just another kid, like, maybe, even a friend. But at the moment, it seemed she was sliding into the "pity" group.

CHAPTER THIRTEEN

The Things Money Can't Buy

After school, instead of pulling out my tape measure, I just sat on the bed staring at the neat row of inches on the tape. Would I do this every day for the rest of my life, I wondered. When I grow up and get a job, will I come home from work to this very same room and pull out this very same tape measure to find out . . . what? That my arms and legs are two different lengths?

"Say that box was for you," I said to my mother as we were driving around town a few days later. "What would need to be in it so you would feel as happy as Sarah did when she opened hers?"

"Oh, I don't know. When you get to be my age, you can buy things. Things don't contribute much to my happiness."

"But I'm not your age," I said. "And I can't think of anything, either."

"What about an inch each for your arm and your leg?"

"I don't know. Maybe."

"Just think. You'd be regular. You'd be like everybody else."

"Like everybody else," I repeated.

And for some reason I thought about Glynnis Powell just then. And how unlike everyone else she was: so crisp and tidy in appearance, her handwriting neat enough to frame. The way

134

her bangs lined up in an even fringe beneath her kerchief, you just knew she had serious things on her mind.

The other day when I shined my quarters for her, her cheeks tinged pink and she whispered, "Thank you, Franklin, for the 100 percent organic fruit roll," not directly to me but down at her hands. Her hands with the nails that shone like little slivers of moon.

Being regular just didn't have the same appeal for me once I remembered all that about Glynnis.

There was one more big surprise coming for Sarah Kervick. Two days before the Pelican View Ice and Fitness Center was scheduled to open, my mother made an announcement.

"I know a guy who can sharpen your new skates," she said. "Better bring 'em with you to practice. And bring a sweater, too. It's like the Penguin House at the zoo in that place."

"Will we see the ice?" Sarah wanted to know. "Is the rink frozen yet?"

My mother had promised to take us to the first open skate.

"They're working on it," was all she said.

But when we got there, she took us right into the rink. There it was: a huge field of ice. The surface was smooth and glassy and beautiful.

"Can I touch it?" Sarah asked with awe.

"Well, the thing is . . ." My mother glanced at Sarah and me, drawing out the moment. She was up to something. Something good, from the way she was smiling.

"They're having a skating party tonight for all the big donors. See how smooth it is? My friend Paul used to operate the forklift over at Megamart, but now he works here, driving the Zamboni. See, after a lotta people go on the ice, you have to smooth it out. Even after one person goes on the ice, you need to smooth it out some. He's comin' by later this afternoon to smooth it out for the party and all—" She broke off and started to laugh.

"You just don't get it, do you, Sarah? It's your turn now. All by yourself. Paul is one of those wonderful strangers that Gloria was telling you about. He's gonna come in and clean up later, so you can skate on this rink right now all by yourself."

Sarah threw her arms around my mother. "Didya hear it, Franklin? It's just like a dream. I got the whole place to myself."

Yes, I'd heard it. But just barely. Mentally, I was adding up the number of times my mother had used the name Paul that day. At breakfast: "Paul's got a miter box. He's gonna help me frame in that alcove by the sink there." And at the gas station: "Paul thinks I'd get better gas mileage if I fiddled with the tire pressure. Might get me in good with the boss."

I didn't need a calculator to tell me that you mention someone's name in direct proportion to the amount of time you spend thinking about him. What I did need was at least seven minutes to process what this meant for our family health profile. But there was too much going on at the moment.

We were about to launch Sarah Kervick onto the ice, and despite the fact that she always got to be the one to have the adventures and that this was beginning to be a sore point with me, I wanted to see it.

I had to pay attention. Gloria would be counting on me to cheer her up with a report of this historic moment.

"How much time we got?" Sarah asked breathlessly. "Don't you wanna do somethin' to my skates?"

"No, honey, that was just a little trick to get you to bring them down here. Gloria took care of all that." Consulting her watch, my mother said: "Almost two hours."

Sarah sighed with pleasure. Then she tore open the box and got out her skates. Heads bent together, Sarah and my mother did the laces.

"They should be tight. You don't want them to wobble. But they shouldn't cut off your circulation, either. Here, I'll hold your skate guards." My mother took the long plastic sheaths and stuffed them into the pocket of her jacket.

Sarah squeezed my arm and I didn't even flinch. I was actually starting to get used to all this touching. "Are you gonna watch me, Franklin?"

"Sure, I'll watch," I said, wishing I'd brought a video camera. Gloria would be near to ecstatic if I got a video of this.

In just the same way she seemed to do everything, Sarah Kervick didn't hesitate on the edge of this dream moment. She didn't stop and think about what a big deal this was. What she did was walk carefully to the edge of the rink and launch herself onto the ice, her arms flung out wide, like she was expecting some invisible force to catch her if she fell. And she did fall. Over and over.

I guess dreaming doesn't teach you balance.

Once she was on her feet again, she'd take off, digging her toes in the ice and doing this funny tiptoe thing until she lost her balance and fell forward again.

"She's too greedy," my mother said, watching her. "It's like she's trying to eat the experience rather than just have it."

She stuck her fingers in her mouth and produced the same shrill whistle that called Sarah in from the outfield. Sarah walked, slipped, and toppled over to the railing at the edge of the rink.

"I don't know much about skating," my mother said, "but I figure you can't think of it like walking. Slow down, push back and away from the center of your body."

To demonstrate, my mother moved her feet like she was dancing. "You're in too much of a hurry."

"Okay," Sarah said, panting. Her cheeks were flushed, and in the big fluffy sweater that hid her bony arms, she definitely looked regular. I'd even say she looked pretty.

"Franklin, it's so fun!" she called up to me. "It's just how I imagined it."

And I knew right then, no matter what, that Sarah Kervick was going to be all right. I think I even understood just how it was she kept going. All those days she spent sliding in the dust in front of her trailer, she was seeing this moment. And now, she was seeing the moment when she would glide across the ice like a pro. I admired Sarah for that. She had one good imagination.

"I still have some work to do," my mother said, pulling out her receipt pad. "Seems they get little wavy lines when they try to watch the Fitness Channel. You know that won't do. I'll be back in a couple minutes."

Sarah clink, clink, clinked back to the middle of the rink. Holding her arms in front of her as if she were clasping a giant ball, she straightened up and pushed off with one skate. Not bad.

I rubbed my hands together. Even with my long-sleeved underwear and my PrimaLoft jacket, I could not get rid of the chill. Some part of my frozen brain thought of the hot chocolate machine in the lobby. Maybe it wouldn't matter, just this once, if I drank a beverage that was sure to contain hydrogenated vegetable oil. Other kids did it every day, and I didn't see them dropping like flies.

I looked up to see my mother returning with an enormous shopping bag.

"I almost forgot. Sarah's not the only one who gets surprises." She was smiling. "I'm your mom, Franklin. It would mean a lot to me to find the thing that would make you as happy as those skates made Sarah."

She began pulling heavy chunks of molded plastic out of the bag.

"I'm not sayin' this is it," she added, "but if you want to join her . . ."

It was a goalie's uniform, from the head cage to the enormous padded gloves to the shieldlike shin guards. All piled up, the pieces of the uniform were higher than me as I sat there in the bleachers. From the bottom of the bag, she pulled out a pair of battered brown skates.

"A girl I work with over in Montcalm County has a son in hockey," she said. "He outgrew all this, so she let us borrow it. Coach did mention a hock—" She broke off and looked at me.

I leaned over and picked up the skates.

"I disinfected them," my mother said.

But that wasn't what I was thinking. I was thinking that they surely weren't as graceful as Sarah Kervick's. They seemed like the kind of skates that might belong to Marvin Howerton. Like they'd had some experiences from which they were lucky to come out alive.

"Want to try? I could help you on with this stuff."

I looked over the impressive pile of protection and then back out at Sarah on the ice. She had already improved. Her back straight as a ruler, she made her way slowly across the ice, the blades of her skates peeling off layers rather than chunks.

"I think I'll watch for a little while," I said.

She patted my shoulder and looked across the ice to Sarah's figure.

"She's going to get good, isn't she? She's going to make that ice behave."

"She'll beat it into submission," I agreed, as if such a thing were possible.

"Well, I told 'em I just had to make this little delivery to you, so I better get back."

I watched Sarah for a while longer.

What was it like to be fearless?

"The only thing we have to fear is fear itself." It was FDR's voice that delivered the familiar line in my ear. I almost saw him there, sitting next to me in his big wool overcoat and muffler, patting me with a giant mittened hand.

Go on, son, he was saying. *It's not just a bunch of campaign hooey. I really mean it.*

A pair of thick socks tumbled from the bag under my feet. I unrolled them and pulled them on over my own socks. It took a little time to work my feet into the skates, since they were waiting for some other kid's feet. My frozen fingers struggled to tie the laces tight, and I held on for dear life as I climbed down the bleachers.

Hobbling over to the opening of the rink, I was surprised by Sarah, who careened around the bend, tilting at a dangerous angle.

"Franklin?" Breathless, she nearly slid into me as she fell on her butt trying to come to a stop. "Are you comin' out here?"

I decided not to look down at the ice. Its ability to absorb shock seemed woefully inadequate. My teeth started to chatter.

"I could help you, if you want," she offered, holding out her hands.

"P-p-pull me fast," I said, before I could lose my nerve.

I grabbed on to her hands.

"I w-w-want to feel like I'm flying."

Books are so personal. Even when they are filled with characters we have created, a writer's memories are delicately woven into her fictions. When I was about eight years old, for example, a little girl named Sarah showed up in our classroom. Her long blond hair was so tangled, it looked like a robin's nest was perched on the back of her head. I was too polite to ask about it, but I was very curious. After a week or so, the tangles were gone. Someone had combed them out. I'd like to acknowledge that person, but I don't know who he or she is. A teacher? A neighbor? A mother, suddenly come to her senses? Who took the time to notice a little girl's distress and act in order to make her feel better? So, thank you, whoever you are, and thank you to all adults who help children with their generous acts of kindness.

In her letter to Sarah, Gloria says, *"Hold fast to your dream, Sarah. . . . And surround yourself with people who believe in that dream for you. And you will achieve it."*

My dream has been to write books for children, and I've always been careful to surround myself with people who would support me in my dream. The most steadfast among them is my husband, Roger. I've always felt that with Roger, all things are possible. And with my sons and my wonderful friends and family, I am blessed with support. I'd also like to thank my mom and dad, Joan and Al Stauffacher, for teaching me how good it feels to help someone in need, and my mother-in-law, Marge Gilles, and my friends Debra and Levitan for cheering on *Donuthead* from the first draft.

My agent, Wendy Schmalz, has been representing me for

many years. After a dry period with no sales, I asked Wendy why she didn't dump me in favor of more lucrative clients. She said, "Because I believe in you, that's why." I will be forever grateful for her friendship and her faith in me.

Finally, I don't think people realize the extent to which a writer and an editor collaborate to create a book. When I met Nancy Hinkel, my editor at Knopf, I knew that Donuthead had found a wise and witty companion on his journey to becoming a novel. Nancy challenged me to write a better story, and her suggestions resulted in enhancements I wouldn't have dreamed possible. If you like Paul, Bernie, Glynnis, even dented packages of Twinkies, then know you have Nancy to thank for this. I know I do. It has been a wonderful experience to collaborate on Donuthead with such a gifted editor.

• • •